"You Can't Escape
What's Going to Happen Between Us."

"Nothing is going to happen."

He braced his arms on either side of her head, leaning closer and closer. With the merest tilt of her head, he would have access to her lips.

"No, Damon."

"Yes, Tamara."

"The vice president of the school board and a teacher? A teacher who earns extra money by—"

He stole the last word with a hard kiss. "A man and a woman."

With superhuman will, she ducked beneath his arm, opened the car door and slid behind the wheel. "I'm not prepared for the consequences."

Dear Reader,

Welcome to Silhouette! Our goal is to give you hours of unbeatable reading pleasure, and we hope you'll enjoy each month's six new Silhouette Desires. These sensual, provocative love stories are both believable and compelling—sometimes they're poignant, sometimes humorous, but always enjoyable.

Indulge yourself. Experience all the passion and excitement of falling in love along with our heroine as she meets the irresistible man of her dreams and together they overcome all obstacles in the path to a happy ending.

If this is your first Desire, I hope it'll be the first of many. If you're already a Silhouette Desire reader, thanks for your support! Look for some of your favorite authors in the coming months: Stephanie James, Diana Palmer, Dixie Browning, Ann Major and Doreen Owens Malek, to name just a few.

Happy reading!

Isabel Swift
Senior Editor

JO ANN ALGERMISSEN
Naughty, but Nice

Silhouette Desire

Published by Silhouette Books New York

America's Publisher of Contemporary Romance

SILHOUETTE BOOKS
300 E. 42nd St., New York, N.Y. 10017

Copyright © 1985 by Jo Ann Algermissen

Distributed by Pocket Books

ISBN: 0-373-05246-4

First Silhouette Books printing November 1985

10 9 8 7 6 5 4 3 2 1

America's Publisher of Contemporary Romance

Printed in the U.S.A.

JO ANN ALGERMISSEN

believes in love, be it romantic love, sibling love, parental love or love of books. She's given and received them all. Ms. Algermissen and her husband of twenty years reside in Houston, Texas, along with their two children, a weimaraner and three horses. She considers herself one lucky lady.

Dedicated, with heartfelt gratitude, to
Tara Hughes,
whose special brand of encouragement
and understanding made writing this book possible.

One

***

The Foxx is in the henhouse!''

The whispered warning from the school switch-board operator had the same effect as a spitball whizzing past her ear as she wrote the daily assignment on the blackboard. Tamara Smith grimaced.

Each teacher who passed her doorway was given the same coded message. Their reactions were much the same as they hustled to their last class. Within minutes, the entire building would be prepared for the "surprise" visit.

Why is he here? Tamara silently asked. She locked her classroom door. Seventh period was her free period. Did the Foxx know? Her back teeth ground together. The Foxx knew everything, good, bad or indifferent, that took place within the boundaries of the Baylor Independent School District.

Tamara clenched her daily lesson plan book protectively to her chest. Assuming he knew about the afterschool seminar she and Melissa Hawkins conducted, she briskly strode to Melissa's door.

"Did you hear?"

Melissa silently bobbed her head up and down. "We're going to be observed, aren't we?"

Hearing the tremor in her co-worker's voice, Tamara gave her a comforting hug. "We're legal. Don't worry."

"Don't worry? Don't worry, the lady says," Melissa repeated incredulously. "You and I both know the Foxx wields the ax in the henhouse. When the staff is reduced, you also know who's going to be first in line at the chopping block!"

Tamara laughed at Melissa's dramatic hand gesture as it made a hacking motion across her own throat. "We're safe. The curriculum and the seminar are approved. Mama Hen can protect her little chick."

"Mama hens are the first ones to get the ax," Melissa cautioned.

The tardy bell rang.

Tamara winked at Melissa as she closed the door. Her brave facade crumbled as her brow pleated into a worried scowl. This wasn't the first time she had been in trouble. Baylor City residents kept a wary eye in her direction. But for appearance's sake, Tamara flaunted her reputation under their upturned noses.

She turned a deaf ear to their suspicions, never letting any of them have the satisfaction of knowing how their sharp tongues wounded her. They expected her to be naughty. And she didn't disappoint them.

Under normal circumstances, she would have headed to the teacher workroom to begin preparing next week's lesson plans. Instead Tamara headed for the teacher's lounge. Administrators considered the lounge a hotbed of insurrection. They expected her to spend her preparation period rabble-rousing. Tamara grinned.

The nearly empty lounge was a double disappointment. The Foxx wasn't in the room, but Emma and Bertha Schultz were.

"Ladies?" Her tone reflected her surprise at their gracing the lounge. Or possibly it questioned the meaning of the standard greeting. "The Foxx is here."

Her grin became a full-fledged smile as she watched them flurry around the room, picking up their materials. The Schultz sisters had a reputation, also. The maiden schoolmarms, thanks to their impeccable birthright, were pillars of the community.

"We came in to get a soda pop," Emma explained. "Our throats were parched."

Tamara shrugged. "Teachers are entitled to a few moments of relaxation."

The blasphemy made both of the elderly women gasp. "Not in this district!" Emma crisply announced. Bertha gave a sharp nod of agreement as she followed her sister out of the austere lounge.

Tamara's blue eyes sparkled with silent laughter. She poured herself a cup of coffee and sat down by the telephone. The fragrant steam from the cup was enticing, but Tamara wasn't surprised by the bitter, strong flavor. It had been brewing since early morning.

She glanced over her shoulder at the door, contemplating the risk of making a personal phone call. Lizzie Compton, a retired teacher, knew she had the last period of the day off, and would be anxiously waiting. Disregarding the risk factor, Tamara dialed her number.

"Lizzie, it's all scheduled," she said in a low tone, once initial pleasantries had been exchanged. "I'm not promising he'll be a football star, but Mickey can take care of you."

"You're a sweetheart! Do I pay you or Mickey?"

"Pay him for his services if you're satisfied. Then drop a check in the mail for me."

"I wouldn't have the nerve to drive to Houston at night by myself for the revival," she confided. "You know how the muggers thrive on little old ladies!"

Tamara chuckled. "Lizzie, I promise. You aren't going to be robbed, raped or pillaged. Mickey will protect you." She heard the soft click of the lounge door. Surreptitiously she glanced over her shoulder. Her eyes widened. Clearing her throat and adopting a businesslike voice, she concluded, "Mickey is a

hard-working student. I'm certain he'll satisfactor-
ily complete the assignment."

"Somebody there?"

"Yes, ma'am. If you need detailed information
regarding the assignment, please don't hesitate to call
me at home."

"Thanks, Tamara."

"My pleasure. Our district prides itself on the
achievement of each student," she added for good
measure. The favorite phrase the administrators used
this year harped on individualized instruction.
"'Bye."

The Foxx was plunking quarters into the Coke
machine, but Tamara noticed his reddish-tinged head
was cocked in her direction. *Let him stick that in his
policy handbook,* she mused as she hung up the
phone.

Boldly she watched him reach down to extract a
can from the machine. Every male teacher in the
building wished he'd live long enough to afford an
expensive, tailored, three-piece suit like the one the
Vice President of the Baylor City School Board wore.
Her eyes strayed from the knife-sharp crease of the
slacks to the width of his muscular shoulders. Ruefully she silently admitted that she admired more
than the cut of his suit.

Years ago, when she had been seated in the rows
facing the teacher's desk, she had mooned over Damon Foxx. He was everything she wasn't. Class
president. Football star. Wealthy. Respectable. Tamara hadn't forgotten how she'd caught him watch-

ing her, but he didn't allow the attraction to extend as far as asking her out.

"Tamara," he said, officially acknowledging her presence. "Good to see you."

"Thank you, sir," she responded, with the respect his position required.

He gestured to the phone as he folded his tall frame into a straight-backed chair beside the table. "The patrons of the district appreciate having the staff available after school hours. That was a good piece of public relations I overheard."

"I'm available when I'm needed." Tamara watched a pinkish tinge color his neck and the line of his square jaw. She smiled, recalling being fascinated by a similar flush ten years earlier. Then she realized his obvious interpretation of her well-meant words. Her smile faded. He still expected her to behave like the "naughty girl of Baylor High." Her dark-fringed eyes narrowed fractionally.

"The school board doesn't expect all your nighttime activities to center on your job."

"They don't. I'm dedicated, but..." She purposely put her hands to her neck and provocatively stretched. Her eyes beckoned his to follow their path as she lowered them over her feminine curves, which were professionally covered in a navy blue suit. "But I don't wear a hair shirt."

Damon hooked his index finger beneath his starched collar. The flush swept to his high cheekbones. "Silk blouse instead of a, er, sweater."

Tight sweater, Tamara wanted to supply, but didn't. Evidently she wasn't the only one in the lounge who had taken a quick stroll down Memory Lane. For a second she was ashamed of losing control and letting her teenage automatic defense mechanism take over. *Inexcusable,* she chastised. She'd learned several harsh lessons because of being born in Pickler Park, but the "naughty girl" attitude had matured into a socially acceptable icy, cool demeanor.

"Did you want something?" she inquired in a frosty voice.

Damon grinned. "I've had a couple of calls about you."

"Oh?"

"Fred Roberts called regarding his daughter's books being *rained* on in her locker."

"Ah yes, Fred contacted me, also. He was distressed. He objected to paying for the ruined textbook."

"Why didn't you issue a free copy?"

Tamara reached over to the table, and picked up the policy book Damon had put there. "The book says, and I quote: 'Students are responsible for all materials issued by the district—'"

"'And shall be charged for any excessive deterioration,'" Damon recited, without benefit of the manual.

"The book was ruined."

"You were informed of the leak in the roof."

"Actually I filed a hazard report weeks ago. The rainwater also runs down the back wall of my classroom. Dangerously close to an electrical outlet." She snapped the book shut. "Nothing was done."

Prior to visiting the lounge, Damon had spoken to the principal about the leak, but ethics prohibited him from informing a staff member that an administrator had already been chewed out. "So to draw attention to the problem, you gave my name to Fred."

"Incorrect, Mr. Foxx," she replied formally. "The problem was beyond my jurisdiction. Shall I read the fine print on the last page of the handbook?"

"'Feel free to contact a board member...' et cetera, et cetera, et cetera?"

"With the phone numbers listed." Tamara shot him a wide-eyed, innocent look.

"I received the call at midnight."

Tamara barely restrained a chuckle over that tasty morsel of poetic justice. She didn't have enough fingers and toes to count the number of times her phone had rung in the middle of the night regarding school business.

"I hope he didn't interrupt anything. I suggested that Fred call you at home rather than at the real-estate office, but I didn't specify how late. I hope you didn't lose any sleep."

"Point taken, Tamara," he murmured. "My second caller was anonymous."

She audibly groaned, but refrained from rolling her eyes to the ceiling to call on a higher being to give her patience. "The S-E-X seminar," she whispered, imitating the panting of an obscene phone caller.

"Precisely."

"Precisely what?" she demanded. "This battle was fought before you were elected to the school board. The guidelines for the pilot program were approved."

"The person who called was concerned about an unmarried woman conducting the class."

Exasperated by the early-nineteenth-century attitude, Tamara rose to her feet. "What did the old biddy say? Watch out! She's teaching immorality to our youngsters. She's providing them with maps of all the isolated county roads behind Pickler Park. She's giving them free passes to the drive-in theater. Give me a break, Damon!"

Damon leaned back in his chair, away from the unexpected outburst. Her blue eyes sparked with the same fire he'd seen years ago when the Pickler Park contingency of the high school had challenged the dress code. He recalled the painted-on tightness of the jeans, the saucer-sized sunglasses and the snug red sweater she'd worn. The school board had been right to suspend them for disrupting classes. He could certainly have attested to being unable to concentrate on anything other than Tamara Smith.

"I'm here as an impartial observer," he replied mildly.

"You're here to judge! Isn't one judge in your family enough? I know you left town for several years, but I didn't know you'd received a law degree!'' By the time she swung around to physically confront him, the endearing, involuntary flush had reached the roots of his dark auburn hair. "I apologize," she hastily muttered.

Damon slowly rose to his feet. Scant inches separated them. "The board neither expects you to work twenty-four hours a day nor wear a chastity belt. I'm not here to put your neck on the chopping block, Tamara," he stated in a gentle voice.

Startled by his choice of imagery, she wondered if he knew about the teachers' code.

He nodded as though he had heard her voice the silent question. Because she was riled up, he didn't feel this was the time to broach the subject of the final accusation the anonymous caller had made. In fact, he'd slammed the phone down on the receiver when the whispered tone claimed Tamara Smith was selling the services of local college boys to dirty old women.

Gathering up her plan book, Tamara fought the urge to flee. Her entire life she'd fought malicious gossip and innuendos. Hadn't she paid the price for respectability by teaching in the district the past four years? Keeping her nose clean by placing it against the grindstone wasn't enough? She empathized with the majority of Pickler Park teenagers who moved out of Baylor City the moment the ink dried on their driver's licenses.

Not me! Her rounded chin jutted forward. *They'll never run me off. I'll fight them to my last breath!*

Forcing her vocal cords to respond in a controlled voice, she asked, "Is that all, Mr. Foxx?"

Damon lightly touched her arm. "I'm not going to hurt you," he said when he saw her flinch. "The board being kept ignorant of what goes on causes a state of turmoil, not a state of bliss."

Her head raised as she scanned his expressive face for condescension. "I'm a professional. Your being here, observing the seminar, smacks of distrust."

"We're both doing our jobs," he replied, justifying his presence.

Too true, Tamara thought. The only difference was that he could afford to donate his time to the community while she was being paid for her services. Although they were close enough to kiss, the gap between them was wider than the railroad tracks separating his side of town from hers.

"I'll expect to see you after school," she conceded. The inevitable couldn't be postponed. She managed a weak smile to lighten the tension between them. "Who knows? You might learn something."

He dropped his hand from her arm, fingers burning. Damon had a gut-level feeling Tamara Smith could teach him things that weren't in the curriculum guide. The question whether he would be an apt pupil was yet to be decided.

"Issue Fred's daughter a new book, please."

The politeness of the request couldn't be misconstrued as an order. Tamara nodded. She turned toward the door.

"Tamara."

His voice seemed to echo out of the past. Her steps faltered. Warily she glanced over her shoulder.

"It was good talking to you."

She drew a long breath, but couldn't get any words past the lump forming in her throat. Another weak smile parted her lips, indicating she'd heard him.

As she closed the lounge door behind herself, she wanted to vent her frustration by scoffing at his charm. Dammit, did he have to be...nice! Fighting someone who couldn't look her in the eye because his nose was scraping the clouds, she could handle, but fighting someone who steadily gazed into her eyes was tough.

"He can get you fired!" she mumbled, whipping up her defenses. She wasn't protected by the Texas tenure law. It took five years, not four, to secure her job. The threat of dismissal hung heavily over her head.

Back in her room she pulled the Encounter games out of the storage cabinet. Maybe she should have played it safe and not volunteered to conduct the seminars. Naiveté wasn't a viable explanation for her decision. She was well aware of the risks. The narrow-minded townspeople still suspected her withdrawal from high school her senior year and her prolonged stay in Houston were due to being *caught*. She set the games on the tables around the classroom.

The antiquated term "caught" reflected their Civil War attitudes toward the sexual revolution more clearly than the Confederate flag hanging on the back wall between the American and Texas flags. Pride kept her from rebutting the vicious rumor. Pride in herself and family pride. She and her mother knew it was her cousin who had had the unplanned pregnancy. Had her mother been physically able, she would have gone to Houston. The vicious rumor would have been avoided. The truly ironic twist of the unwanted pregnancy was that Martha had been married. Because of financial stress and four other children, Martha had seriously considered abortion. During a prolonged bout of depression, she'd called Tamara and asked for help.

Tamara didn't regret transferring from Baylor City High. Family pride prohibited her giving a reason for leaving. But to this day, she could vividly remember the expression on the head cheerleader's face when she returned her uniform. Mistakenly Tamara had thought the tears rolling down both their faces had expressed mutual sadness over her untimely departure. It wasn't until she returned to Baylor City that she discovered they had been tears of pity. The entire town thought she had given birth to an illegitimate child. In the privacy of her own home, she had shed more tears over the injustice, but no one had ever known how deeply those sly, accusing stares had wounded her.

Her lips tugged downward as she opened the game board at the last table. And now she was educating the youngsters about sex. Had she intentionally placed this stumbling block between herself and gaining tenure? Did the person who made the phone call to Damon think she was still flinging their sexual mores into their faces? Again they were wrong. But the satisfaction of knowing they were wrong didn't change anything.

Nothing had changed. The whole town would have to be leveled by the forces of nature before anything changed. And the likelihood of that happening were as remote as Tamara's being offered a fifth contract.

"Then why are you batting your head against a brick wall?" she whispered. "The kids need to be educated" was her immediate, forceful response to her own question. In particular, the students from Pickler Park needed someone from their own streets to look up to. They needed a role model, and Tamara was it.

Later, halfway through the seminar, Melissa nudged Tamara and glanced at the doorway. Damon Foxx openly watched her. The room seemed to shrink in size. There wasn't a cranny anywhere large enough to hide in to get away from his dark amber-colored eyes. Finally she crooked her finger, beckoning him into the classroom.

"Mr. Foxx, would you like to see how the game is played?" she invited cordially. "I believe you know Mrs. Thomas and her daughter Maxine, and Mr. Cromwell and his son Mark. Mark, why don't you explain the rules of the game while I help another table?"

Tamara smiled and politely excused herself. Slowly she circled each table, commenting, laughing, encouraging when necessary. By the time she returned to the table where Damon was seated, only ten minutes were left in the seminar.

"Six! That puts you right here on an exclamation point!" Mark announced, moving his father's marker. "Draw!"

Somewhat apprehensively Damon reached for the stack of yellow cards in the center of the board. "I volunteered to take Mr. Cromwell's turn," he explained to Tamara.

"Read it aloud," Mark razzed, thoroughly enjoying the game.

"'Where do you hear sex talked about most often: a) at home, b) at school, c) with friends of the same sex, or d) with friends of the opposite sex?'"

Tamara grinned at the way his brow furrowed in consternation.

"In all honesty I have to answer, at school," Damon replied.

"Wow! Did they have sex classes way back then?" Mark inquired innocently.

Damon felt his skin begin to betray him as a dark stain colored his cheekbones. "Boys' locker room," he blurted.

"How about that?" Mr. Cromwell pounded Damon jovially on the shoulder. "He took the same class I did. That classroom was one step to the right of the gymnasium and directly under the flight path of the stork," he informed his son with false sincerity.

"Want to take my turn?" Mrs. Thomas asked, holding the dice out for Tamara to take.

"Go ahead," Damon encouraged. "Let's see if you're qualified to teach this seminar."

"Yeah. We'll pretend you're Mr. Foxx's mother," Mark suggested with a mischievous twinkle in his eyes.

She rolled the dice to draw the attention back to the game and away from herself. "Snake eyes."

She groaned as Mrs. Thomas moved her marker to within one block of a ladder that would make her the winner, but she fell short, landing on the same exclamation point Mr. Cromwell's had landed on. Mrs. Thomas handed Tamara a card.

"Here goes nothing. The card asks, 'What is the most effective means of birth control?' Whew! An easy one. The Pill."

"Right," Mr. Cromwell agreed, checking the answer in the manual. "Guess they'll have to update this version of the game when the manufacturers come out with a once-a-month shot for men. Mark, did you hear the commercial about the sponge on the television?"

Tamara listened to the easy flow of conversation between father and son. The goals of the program were being accomplished. Basic information was being exchanged without embarrassment or misinformation being imparted. A strong bond between the teenager and the parent was being forged. A small smile of satisfaction curved her lips upward as she met Damon's eyes.

A squeal from across the room broke their eye contact. Without getting up, she knew one of the mothers' tokens was slithering down a chute. Glancing at her watch, she rose to her feet and walked to the center of the room.

"Ladies. Gentlemen." She paused and waited for the room to quiet. "Thanks for coming. Next month there will be a father-son panel discussing the importance of values in a dating relationship."

Melissa piped up from the back of the room, "We've called this session, 'Hard Rock versus Easy Listening.' On that happy note, let us thank you for coming. We'll look forward to seeing you next month."

While the games on each table were being put away, Tamara and Melissa talked individually to the parents before they departed. By the time the room cleared, and Tamara had a chance to ask Damon his opinion on the seminar, he was no longer in the room. She sighed, disappointed.

"Good session," Melissa commented. "What did the Foxx think of it?"

"He joined in. I'm disappointed he didn't stick around to let us know what he thought."

"I did," Damon said as he stepped from the hallway into the room. "One of the parents wanted to discuss the bidding system on contracting labor for the district. The Foxx," he gently jibed, smiling crookedly in Melissa's direction, "thinks the students are fortunate to have two such *capable* ladies in the henhouse. In fact, it would be my pleasure to

take both of you out for dinner to discuss imple-
menting this pilot program throughout the district."

While Melissa strangled on the code phrase, Tamara glowed under his praise.

"Can't. But thanks, anyway," Melissa managed
to sputter.

"How about you, Tamara?"

"Tonight is our bowling league night. Melissa and
I bowl on the same team."

"Great! I haven't bowled since my college days.
Why don't you change clothes, and we'll grab a
quick bite to eat, then I'll come with you and
watch?"

"It's the teachers' league."

"So? Some of my best friends are teachers," he
teased lightly.

Tamara felt as though she was being steamroll-
ered by his high-spirited enthusiasm. What was it
about this man's lopsided grin that warmed her
bones, made her knees weak? She couldn't take him
to the bowling lanes.

"We could discuss the pilot program between
hamburger bites and throwing the bowling ball," he
coaxed, seeing her hesitancy.

And afterward, she wondered. Tamara rested one
hip on the corner of the desk. Remembering the last
faculty meeting when the principal, Mr. St. Cyr, reprimanded the teachers who leaned, draped or vul-
garly displayed themselves by sitting on the desk, she
hastily straightened.

"I'm not the enemy," Damon reassured. He watched her shake her head and decline the invitation. "Another time?"

"Lizzie offered to get tickets for the Manilow Concert..." Melissa suggested.

"Melissa!" All Tamara needed would be Damon talking to Lizzie and finding out she was moonlighting. Board members vehemently opposed jobs away from the school. Her name would be at the top of the reduction-in-staff list if they discovered the escort service. The glare she shot her teammate softened when she noticed the slight blush sweeping up Damon's neck. "Thanks for the invitation, but it's impossible."

"Maybe two years from now, when I'm off the school board?"

Tamara grinned. Damon wasn't obtuse. He didn't need a flashing tally sheet to know the score.

Shoving both hands in his pockets, he nodded his head, accepting his defeat graciously. "Thanks for allowing me to participate in the game. 'Night, ladies."

"'Night," Melissa and Tamara chimed.

Both women watched him stride through the doorway. Tamara reached over and tapped Melissa beneath her jaw. "You're gaping."

"I'm astounded. Do you realize you just turned down a date with the most eligible bachelor in Baylor City?" Melissa slapped her forehead dramatically. "And he's rich, rich, rich! He's in every Pickler Park girl's dreams!"

"Damon Foxx is vice president of the school board," Tamara pointedly retorted. "Strictly a hands-off, off-limits community hero."

Two

Damon drove from his Main Street office building toward his house. Defensively he blinked, glancing to the side of the street as an oncoming car sped through town with its lights on high. The winking neon sign of the bowling lanes caught his attention. Lucky Lanes was the only bowling establishment in town. As though the car were on automatic pilot, the steering wheel smoothly swerved to the right, into the parking lot.

He opened the door, glancing at his watch. The early league should be finishing their last game, he surmised, as he strode through the double doors.

The noise from balls rolling down the alleys, striking pins, and the soft music wafting into the dimly lit twenty-four-lane building were unfamiliar, and he began to feel uncomfortable about his impulsive decision to drop by. Where he stood was comparatively dark, but the approach to the lanes was brightly lit.

He honestly didn't know what compelled him to seek out a woman who bluntly refused to be seen with him. At thirty-two, he was a bit old to be chasing after someone who declined a date not once but twice. His stomach growled, signaling an internal rebellion against his skipping dinner.

He glanced at the overhead score boards, scanning them for her name. He recognized several staff members of both sexes as they prepared to throw their balls down their respective lanes. Which team was Tamara on? Was she dating one of the male members of the six-person team? Was that why she didn't want him to watch her bowl? He was totally in the dark in more ways than one.

Damon saw Tamara flash a brilliant smile back to her teammates. She picked up a royal blue bowling ball from the carrier. With slow deliberation, she turned toward the pins. Gracefully she approached the foul line, lightly hurling the ball with a force he would have sworn her slender arm wasn't capable of. Arm thrust forward, balanced on one bent leg, back arched, leg extended, she held the classic pose of an expert bowler.

"Woman throws a damned fine curve," Damon commented appreciatively. Not to mention, he silently added, the way she looked poised on one

shapely leg with the upswept arm thrusting her
rounded breasts forward. He suspected Tamara
Smith, once she set her mind on a goal, perfected
everything she did to a high level of competency, be
it work or play. Content with watching, he sat down
at the snack counter directly behind the lane and listened to her teammates cheer the speeding ball down
the lane. The pins exploded upward when it solidly
hit the pocket.

"Strike—that's two!" Melissa shouted. "Our an-
chor lady is tough tonight!"

Damon read the team name stenciled on the back
of her shirt and chuckled to himself. Teach Me Tonight. Tamara Smith could teach him tonight, or any
other night for that matter. A bit of private tutoring
would suit Damon Foxx just fine.

"Can I get you something?" the waitress asked.

He ordered a cheeseburger and fries. Two seconds later, he canceled the onions on the burger.

Tamara snapped her fingers as she heard the neat
click the pins made when perfectly hit. Her team had
lost both of the two previous games because she was
bowling far below her average. Now, finally, she was
back in the groove.

She swiped her hand over the finger blower before she sat on the curved bench near the scorekeeper. Thinking about Damon Foxx had made her rush
her line, grip the ball too tightly and miss her mark
repeatedly. Pangs of guilt over letting her team down
didn't improve her concentration or her score. She'd
disappointed the team.

"Telephone for Tamara Smith. Telephone for Tamara Smith," an anonymous voice over the loudspeaker system paged.

"Who'd be calling you here?" Melissa asked as she watched Tamara glance toward the pay phones situated next to the snack counter.

Tamara shrugged. "If I'm up on the other lane, bowl around me. Okay?"

She hastily climbed the six steps from the lane to the level overlooking the lanes. She hated being called away from the game. It broke her concentration. The waitress held up two fingers and pointed to the line of phones near the counter.

Damon, sitting at the end of the counter, turned away from the lanes when he heard her name announced. He hunched forward, eating his cheeseburger. Tamara came close enough for him to feel a slight breeze as she passed by without recognizing him.

"Hello?" she shouted over the noise. "Who?"

"I'm a friend of Lizzie Carmichael's. I'm sorry to interrupt your bowling game, but I'd like to go to the revival with Lizzie tomorrow night. I wondered if your young man could pick both of us up."

"Two of you? I think that can be arranged," Tamara answered. "But I'll have to up the price nominally to cover his expenses." She could barely hear the soft-spoken woman. She put one finger over her ear and squeezed her eyes shut to block the noise. "Could you speak a little louder?"

"I said, that's fine. Money isn't a problem."

"I don't have a pen and paper handy. Mickey will pick Lizzie up first, then come to your house. Could you give me your name?" Tamara glanced over her shoulder at the scoreboard. She was up next. "Box? Claudia Box?"

"No, dear. Foxx! Claudia Foxx!"

Her lips twitched into a small smile. How obliging of the fates to put her into a situation where Damon's grandmother *needed* her. On second thought, she mused, her lips thinning, he would object to her moonlighting. The tunnel vision of a school board member would not broaden wide enough to view her escort service as solving the problems of elderly women while alleviating the financial pinch of local college students.

Her eyes opened just in time to see Damon Foxx strangling on a bite of his sandwich.

Oh no, she groaned silently. She didn't have to worry about Mrs. Foxx letting her grandson know about her moonlighting. He'd heard the incriminating evidence with his own bright red ears!

"You enjoy yourself, Mrs. Foxx. Be sure to call Lizzie. 'Bye."

In the bright light, Tamara could see the flush on Damon's face. "Caught me moonlighting, didn't you?"

"Moonlighting?" he repeated, struggling to keep from shouting. The thought of his own grandmother involved in a sex scandal paralyzed his tongue. She'd been a respectable widow for years. "I don't believe you're fixing little old ladies up with

young   men   and   innocently   labeling   it
Moonlighting!''

"What?" She wasn't certain she clearly understood his accusation.

"An anonymous caller warned me, but—"

Ten years ago she would have exploded, but not
now. A decade ago she would have flouced down the
steps, swinging her hips provocatively, but not now.
At her worst, she would have sandblasted his already red face with scathing obscenities. She was
boiling mad on the inside, but outwardly she remained poised. The cool exterior she'd cultivated
over the years held her in good stead. "Since you
obviously knew about the service, I gather you rec-
ommended it to your grandmother. Thanks."

His redheaded temper, which he prided himself on
keeping under control, ignited. The color drained
from his face. "I'd like to shake you *and* my grandmother until your teeth rattle!"

"Brawling? In public?" she retorted sweetly. She
leaned closer, loudly whispering, "With a woman?"

"If you were a man, you'd be out on the parking
lot with a set of loose teeth instead of parading
around here with your—" his voice dropped to a
shouted whisper "—*Loose Morals*!"

"*My* morals are beyond reproach, Mr. Foxx. I
suggest you check out your own chicken coop before you start hurling accusations."

Damon rolled to his feet, slapped a couple of green
bills on the counter and ground from between
clenched teeth, "I'll do that. In the meantime, can-

cel your scheduled intimate threesome for my grandmother. She won't be available!"

Leaning toward him, chin thrust upward, eyes glistening, she felt like grabbing him around the waist and holding on until she cleared her name, her reputation. A threesome? With young boys and grandmothers? Her thoughts fragmented at the outrageous slur. She wouldn't waste her breath to give credence to the accusation.

"I'm on to you. And I'll stop you. The last thing my grandmother needs is a—"

"Hush!" Automatically her fingers reached up to his lips. Damon captured her wrist.

"You'd like that, wouldn't you? Involving my grandmother in your illicit scheme—"

"Tamara!" Melissa shouted from the steps leading up from the lanes. "You're up!"

Tugging her wrist free from his grip, Tamara shouted over her shoulder, "I'm coming."

In the half second her head was turned, Damon angrily marched toward the exit.

Dazed, Tamara stood frozen. She couldn't believe his interpretation of the escort service. She folded her arms over her chest as though physically wounded. Briskly she rubbed her chilled forearms.

"Tamara! Last frame!" her teammates chorused.

Her vision blurred as she glanced from the lane to the front door, then back to her friend's faces. Thankful that no one had heard the steamy confrontation between herself and Damon, she strode toward the steps.

Tamara bent her head and picked up her bowling ball, chewing the side of her lower lip to keep tears from spilling down her cheeks. When she aligned her feet with the two center dots on the approach, all she saw was the livid, red expression on his face. She raised her head to face the pins. She focused her eyes on the spots a third of the way down the lane.

"Well, Mr. Damon Foxx," she muttered under her breath, "here's to you."

The ball rolled out of her hand as she followed through. Strength born of suppressed anger propelled the round object forward. The pins didn't have a prayer of standing against the force, or the accuracy. They bowled over with a sharp click.

"That's a turkey! She's H-O-T, hot, hot, hot!" Melissa chanted with delight.

"Turkey," Tamara muttered, finding the bowling term particularly apropos.

She waited impatiently, one hand on her hip and the other tightly clenched, for the pin setter to rack the pins. Hurt pride made a flood of tears threaten to wash away her anger. Tamara gulped their saltiness down her throat.

"Don't make a spectacle of yourself by bawling," she mouthed, keeping her back to her teammates.

She retrieved the ball from the carrier and charged the line. Her stride lengthened. A buzzer rang as her foot slid over the foul line.

The entire team groaned.

Tamara watched the ball hopscotch down the gutter. She'd blown it. Chagrined, she pivoted and strode off the approach.

"It's okay, Tamara. Pick 'em up. We need the pin count to win," the scorekeeper informed her.

She glanced at the score sheet. A six-point span separated them from winning and losing. Tamara compressed her lips, determined to concentrate on the game and forget Damon Foxx. She couldn't possibly make her average, but she could keep the team in first place by knocking down seven pins.

The ball returned, circling the carrier before she picked it up. Slowly, ever so carefully, she paced the stride of her footsteps down the approach. The moment the ball left her fingertips, she knew she had a good roll. Confident, she grinned as she turned her back on the rolling ball. The dismayed expression on her teammates' faces warned her that all was not going as planned. She turned in time to see the ball plow through the center of the pins. She held her breath, stomped one foot as the four pin wobbled, then finally fell forward. Three other pins stood solid in a six-, seven-, ten-pin split. Long-held air whooshed from between her lips.

Bob grinned. "That's squeaking it through," he congratulated her. "Bet you're glad you don't have to try for that one, aren't you?"

Glancing over her shoulder at the nearly impossible-to-pick split, she nodded her head in agreement. For a second she was glad Damon had stormed out of the building. At least he didn't have the satisfaction of watching her foul up.

"I'll finish," she offered. "You have a wife and kids at home waiting for you."

Rising, Bob held the scorekeeper's chair for her. "Thanks."

Both teams razzed each other as they changed shoes and packed their balls away. No one mentioned Tamara's silence. They knew how a serious bowler felt after a lousy game. Melissa affectionately patted her on the back as the group departed. "Don't be glum. We won!"

The game had been won, but the warfare openly declared by Damon unnerved her.

Tamara averaged each player's scores, noting her average had dropped three pins because of her lousy game. After she changed shoes and turned in the score sheets, she walked through the glass doors. The doors hadn't swung closed when she felt her bowling bag snatched from her hand.

"What are you doing?" she asked in astonishment as she watched Damon shift the suede bag to his other hand, and felt his fingers close around her elbow.

"Being persistent. I'm going to..."

Under the dim light from the low-powered fluorescents, she could see that Damon was still angry. "The full moon tonight is gorgeous," she goaded. "Moonlight..."

"Tell me the truth."

"Why don't I *escort* you to the nearest tavern for a drink?" she provocatively suggested, knowing the board frowned on teachers drinking alcoholic beverages within the school-district boundaries. Her blue eyes sparkled with mischief. She'd bend his rule book around until it resembled a corkscrew. "A double martini?"

"Are you or are you not matching up college kids with female senior citizens?" he growled. His fingers tightened their hold.

Tamara appeared to ponder the outrageous idea. Wounded pride kept her from giving him a straight answer. Evasively she taunted, "I'm actively involved in several community-service projects."

"Tamara," he admonished, "you aren't going to set the record straight, are you?"

Her eyes swept from his russet-colored hair to the tips of his shiny, wing-tipped shoes. "You know, you should have followed in your father's footsteps and become a judge."

"Tamara." The tone of his voice was mockingly aggressive. Effectively, if symbolically, he felt the rule book rapped against his knuckles.

"I haven't violated any rules," she replied sassily.

"Care to share a pot of coffee rather than a shaker of martinis?" he asked, determined to get a straight answer.

She cocked her head, surprised at the invitation. "How about Angelo's café?"

"Fine. My car is over there." He released his hold on her arm, and motioned toward a metal-gray Lincoln.

"I'll lead; you follow," she said, correcting the assumption that she'd allow him to determine the rules governing their relationship. He might as well learn early on that she wasn't the type to be easily picked up and carted off. At Angelo's they'd be on her turf, adhering to her rules.

Damon put her bowling bag in the back seat of her car. Holding the driver's door open for her, he agreed, saying, "Lead the way."

And lead the way she did. Within minutes they were across the tracks, pulling into Angelo's Truck Stop. Tamara grinned. She seriously doubted Damon had ever set foot into the local gathering place for the people at this end of town.

Whatever emotion Damon felt, she couldn't decipher his attitude by looking at his face. Before joining her at the door, he had removed his jacket and rolled up the cuffs of his white shirt. The tie was gone. His unbuttoned collar gaped, revealing thick reddish-brown chest hair.

As she watched his relaxed, athletic stride, she wondered why she mistakenly assumed he would stick out like a sore thumb. He didn't. Put a beer in his hand, lean him up against the counter, and he could be mistaken for one of the locals.

Damon Foxx could adapt to any situation, provided the situation didn't require bending the rules, she decided.

Inside the road-stop café, heads turned as Damon and Tamara entered and seated themselves at a back booth. Several men nudged one another, then grinned.

"Whazzit gonna be?" the waitress asked, sizing Damon up in one all-encompassing sweep of her thickly mascaraed eyes.

"Tamara?"

"The home-made cherry pie is great," she suggested. "And a cup of coffee, Geraldine."

The "who is this hunk" expression on the waitress's face amused Tamara. She grinned and winked at Geraldine. Possessively she ran the fleshy pad of one finger across the knuckles of the man seated across the table from her. In her neighborhood a woman openly claimed a man or he was considered available.

Damon blinked as her finger crossed each bone. His fingers tingled beneath the light touch. "What's going on?" he questioned, once the waitress had lost interest and returned to the kitchen.

A low, throaty chuckle bubbled through her lips. "The rules of the game aren't the same uptown at Tony's?" she teased. "Here, a subtle gesture is sufficient to keep the she-wolves at bay."

"Hmm," he murmured, picking up her hand, drawing the tender flesh of her inner wrist up to brush against his lips. His eyes sparkled mischievously. "Strictly to keep the wolves away."

Tamara arched her eyebrow. "You learn fast."

With a touch softer than fairy wings, his index finger lightly traced a path from her smooth, polished nail to the tiny, sensitive web of each finger. His touch unnerved her. The lopsided grin, the pink tinge climbing up the side of his neck made her breath catch in her throat. Her heart skipped a beat. Damon Foxx was dangerous to her equilibrium.

She withdrew her hand and placed it on her lap.

"So..." The vowel strung out as she sought a safe topic of conversation. "Where did you go after you left the great metropolis of Baylor City?"

"Austin. Houston. San Antonio."

His rust-colored eyes washed over her widow's peak, high cheekbones, uptilted nose, lingering on the full bow of her lower lip.

In a husky voice, Tamara persisted, "Why did you come back?"

"Why did you put your hand in your lap? Scared?"

"Of course not," she denied, willing her voice to contain a certain degree of iciness, but failing. She glanced down. Her left hand followed the path his fingers had taken.

"Hands are a dead giveaway to what a person is like on the inside. Yours are strong and capable. But they are also decidedly feminine...and warm to the touch." His eyes clung to her lips. He heard the soft gasp of air sucked between them. "I wonder—"

"Don't."

"Don't what? Don't contemplate kissing you?" The hand resting on his knee touched the silky flesh of the calf of her crossed leg. When she started as though burned, Damon followed the gentle curve to her delicate ankle.

A tingling sensation traveled from her ankle to her spine, producing a moist, achy feeling in between. Tamara scooted back against the wooden booth. Bending her legs, she crossed her ankles beneath the seat. This wasn't what she'd planned. By bringing him to Angelo's, she'd expected to have the upper hand.

"You mustn't do that," Damon cautioned.

It was her turn to ask "What?"

"Tilt your head a bit, as though you're waiting for my kiss."

Her face felt hot under his scrutiny. Lord, she hoped she wasn't blushing like an eighth grader. Damon made her feel that way: young, innocent, vulnerable.

"What's wrong, Tamara?" He grinned. "Did you think you had your lesson planned and found out you're on the wrong unit? Basic biology instead of constitutional law?" he teased.

"Something like that," she confessed. She had to restore some sort of balance between them. Damon was overpowering her. She felt the icy veneer slipping, melting into a warm moisture, radiating through her bloodstream directly to her heart. "Why did you return to Baylor City?"

Damon leaned back in the wooden booth, aware that now was not the time or place to press his advantage. "It's home. I'd accomplished my objective."

"Which was?" she prompted, determined to keep him talking about himself.

"Seeing if I could make it on my own without benefit of being the son of Judge Foxx," he readily admitted.

"You make it sound as though having Judge Foxx as a father was a handicap."

He shrugged noncommittally. "What keeps you in Baylor City?"

The waitress interrupted to serve the coffee and pie. Tamara welcomed the time to gather her wits before answering. The fragrant hot black coffee gave her an excuse to procrastinate. "Best coffee in town."

"Why?"

The monosyllabic question hung between them.

Tamara knew what she couldn't reveal, but she hesitated, searching for a flippant reply. "Teachers get rich in Baylor City?"

"Sorry. Wrong answer. I know how much you make. Try again."

She picked up her fork and cut into the flaky pie crust. "Basically, I guess we're here for the same reason. It's home."

"Are you living with your mother?"

The tart filling momentarily diverted her attention. "Yes. We now own the house. Between the two of us, we've managed to make it..." She hesitated. Respectable? Her home had always been respectable. Comfortable? With the expensive heating and cooling system, that was appropriate. Beautiful? Tamara grinned. A new paint job and fixing the sagging front porch hardly qualified it for the *Texas Homes* magazine. "Homey."

Damon chewed his food thoughtfully. The stately pillared house he was raised in looked "homey," but if looks dictated appearances, it should have resembled an army barracks. His grandmother's flowerbeds were the single touch of warmth in the entire manicured lawn.

"Here's to being home," he toasted, raising his cup of coffee.

Tamara grinned as she barely tapped the rim of his cup. "When I was a kid, I dreamed of living in a palace." She chuckled. "Funny. Now that I think about it, your house reminds me of what I pictured a princess living in."

"No prince am I," Damon corrected. "I built a house on the outskirts of town. Actually I invested a large percentage of what I earned during the ten years I was away in a ranch eighty miles from town."

"Aha," she teased. "You're drilling for oil. Fits right in with the image." Her slender hand made a panoramic sweep. "South Fork. Oil wells pump out millions from beneath the soil, while cattle lazily graze the pasture. And, in typical J.R. fashion, the owner meddles in local politics."

" 'Fraid not. It's a working ranch, foreman included." He imitated the cherubic grin of J.R.

"Ma'am, I'm not meddling in local politics by being a school-board member."

Tamara sipped her coffee after taking the last bite of cherry pie. "Do you have children in the school system?"

"None."

"A wife who teaches here?"

"No."

"Nieces and nephews?" she asked, extending the scope of the question to prove her point.

"None." Damon lifted one shoulder. "Every kid deserves a good, practical education. When I graduated, I couldn't earn a nickel with the precollege classes I'd taken. That's why I'm backing the trade classes."

"Expensive undertaking," she replied, feeling at ease discussing school problems. "You're going to buy equipment and tools by cutting the teaching staff?"

Damon placed his fork on the plate, wiped his curved lips on a paper napkin. "Ready to leave?"

"You aren't going to answer, are you?"

"I'm not going to discuss the district budget," he agreed, removing his billfold from his breast pocket and paying the tab. "It's after five."

"Didn't Fred Roberts's call at midnight tell you that the school clock doesn't run on Greenwich time? A teacher's day never ends."

"Mine does. You'll be a victim of teacher burnout if you work eighteen hours a day."

"I'll be unemployed if I don't," she blithely contradicted him.

As he rose to his feet, offering his hand to her, he spoke his final word on the subject. "Your job is secure."

Tamara linked her fingers through his and slid out from under the table. Her other hand touched a prominent carving on the corner of the table, drawing her attention downward.

"Do you know that R.M. loves D.F.?" she asked, smiling as she pointed to Damon's initials surrounded by a heart.

"R.M.?" He rubbed his jawline thoughtfully. "'Rebecca Mason?"

"I didn't know you dated her." Her grin widened. Compared to Rebecca Mason, Tamara Smith's reputation was lily-white.

"I didn't."

Her blue eyes rose. Whatever had or had not taken place between Damon and Rebecca, he wasn't going to elaborate. Was his silence indicating his code of chivalry? Or did it exemplify the "cross the tracks to sew your wild oats" attitude prevalent at their high school? The bland expression on his face revealed nothing.

Both of them had questions that the other wouldn't answer. Damon wanted to know about the escort service; she wanted to clarify his attitude about girls from across the tracks.

Neither spoke as they walked side by side, a whisper away from touching, to her car.

"Thanks for the coffee and pie," Tamara politely offered.

"I'll follow you home."

Instead of bidding her good-night, he inched her backward until the car door handle pressed against her spine.

"I know the way. I'm perfectly safe."

Damon bent his head closer. She could smell the aroma of coffee on his breath. "Running?" he whispered.

"Never."

"Liar. You can't escape from what's going to happen between us."

"Nothing is going to happen."

He braced his arms on either side of her head, leaning closer and closer. She knew with the merest tilt of her head, he would have easy access to her lips.

"No, Damon."

"Yes, Tamara," he mocked. He chastely brushed his lips against hers.

"The vice-president of the—" She stopped talking to avoid mumbling the words against his mouth. Electrical sparks ignited between them. Turning her head to the side, she finished "—school board and the teacher? A teacher who earns extra money by—"

He stole the last word with a hard kiss. "A man and a woman."

Tamara shook her head, partly to free herself from his physical hold and partly to shake off the mesmerizing spell he wove. "Uptown and downtown?" she continued.

"A man and woman in an adult situation."

Drawing on her final ounce of willpower, she ducked beneath his arm and opened the car door. Damon stepped back as she slid behind the wheel.

A small, wistful smile curved her lips, taking the sting out of her parting remark. "I'm not prepared for the consequences."

Three

————

Two weeks later, Tamara gracefully ran up the front steps of the administration building. She had successfully avoided Damon Foxx during that time. When her mother answered the telephone, she followed her daughter's instructions to take the name and number. His calls were never returned.

But, tonight she didn't have a choice. As the head of the negotiating team, she was expected to attend each and every board meeting. Tonight was the third Monday of the month, and she was racing to arrive on time.

Without glancing at the men seated at the elevated, long tables at the front of the board room, she picked up the agenda of the meeting off the metal folding chair in the back row of the room and seated herself. The compelling urge to see if Damon was as handsome as she remembered was deliberately squelched by scanning the mimeographed agenda.

Nothing about faculty reduction, she noted, wondering if the board would hold one of the infamous secret meetings after the public board meeting. Tamara needed answers. At the bare minimum, she needed clues as to the general attitude of the board.

Her thoughts scattered as though blown by hurricane force winds when she raised her head, her eyes locking on the devilishly handsome face of Damon Foxx. The dark brown suit contrasted sharply with his white shirt and rust-colored tie. His head inclined a fraction, acknowledging the silent communication between them. One reddish-brown eyebrow slowly rose.

Tamara could almost hear his silent question. "Why didn't you return my calls?"

The lopsided smile accompanying the query reminded her of the same smile she'd seen at Angelo's, when he'd asked her if she was running.

She hadn't been running, she mentally protested. Overly cautious maybe. Exercising wisdom certainly, but Tamara Smith prided herself on facing a problem head-on, never running. If Damon Foxx wished to speak to her about school business, he would have contacted her at work. His attempts to contact her at home put their relationship on a personal level. She was an expert at avoiding personal relationships. Avoiding and running weren't the same, were they?

She rose to pledge allegiance to the flag, which marked the beginning of each meeting. From memory she mouthed the words as she wondered about Damon's conversation with his grandmother. Claudia Foxx had gone with Lizzie, escorted by Mickey, to the revival meeting held in Houston. Smiling, she realized she'd give a week's paycheck to have been a mouse in the corner of the room while that confrontation had taken place. Mrs. Foxx, the grand matriarch of Baylor City, most likely boxed her grandson's ears if he had accused her of having a secret liaison with a college boy. She reseated herself as the meeting was called to order by the president of the board.

Tamara scanned the agenda for the second time. There wasn't anything listed about teachers with part-time jobs, either.

She half listened to the treasurer's report and the various mundane reports covered during the old-business portion of the meeting. She leafed through the stenographer's pad on her lap, checking off each item from the previous meeting. Each time she raised her eyes to the front of the room, she saw Damon watching her.

Although she schooled her face to appear as though she was diligently concentrating on the item under discussion, her finger trembled. What was he doing? The entire room would be following the path of his eyes if he didn't stop. She shook her head, shooting him a meaningful glance.

Damon smiled, momentarily focusing his eyes on the woman who had risen when the president asked for new business. Seconds later, he redirected his attention on Tamara Smith. *God, she's beautiful,* he silently thought. *And I'm off limits,* he added when she shook her head for the second time.

Damon grinned. He might not be able to touch, but by damn, he could look. Somehow, some way, he was going to strip away her mask of iciness and see if the tempestuous Tamara Smith of their high-school days still lurked beneath the surface.

Without his realizing it, his grin widened into a full-fledged smile when he recalled the football team's pet name for her: Queen of the Pizza Hut. Damon swallowed, remembering the dozens of pizzas she'd served him during his senior year. If she realized how much he hated pizza, she would have appreciated more than the tips he'd left. Back then, he'd been too worried about what his father would have thought if he'd brought her home for Sunday dinner. Now? He didn't give a hoot for his father's rules of conduct.

His fingers drummed on the stack of papers beneath them. He softly chuckled aloud when he saw Tamara duck her head behind the man seated in front of her.

What a nincompoop he'd made of himself, he recalled, wondering if she'd refused his calls because of the scene at the bowling lanes. He ruefully added "total" and "raving" to his self-description. But he'd had a tremendous amount of help, thanks to Tamara Smith. She could have told him that she arranged for elderly women who wanted to go to Houston at night to be accompanied by the equivalent of a bodyguard. But she hadn't. She'd practically invited him to think the worst. And, much to his chagrin, he had.

The grating voice of a woman in the front row drew his attention back to the meeting.

"And I don't want unmarried women talking to innocent *children* about sex!" the grim-faced, gray-haired parent concluded indignantly.

Damon reached for the microphone on the table. Glancing at the board president, he flipped up the On switch. "Mrs. Woodward, are you and your child involved in the pilot program?"

"Of course not! But I've heard about what's going on. I know the program will be expanded unless concerned parents object!"

Rising to his feet, Damon picked up the stack of stapled sheets and handed them to the board's secretary. "Would you mind passing these out, please?" He smiled as he turned back to the irate parent. "I personally observed the pilot program two weeks ago. These are my findings."

Tamara caught her breath, tempted to stand up and challenge the inflammatory statement of Mrs. Woodward herself. Although distressed by the woman's tone of voice and lack of valid information, she admired the woman for attending the board meeting and openly voicing her objections rather than participating in the town's whisper campaign.

Before Tamara had a copy of the report in her hands, Damon spoke.

"Mrs. Woodward, the board appreciates your parental concern." His open smile visibly disarmed her. Damon realized she had expected him to be defensive, perhaps belligerent, about her questioning the authority of the board to institute a new program. He watched her eyes drop as they began reading the two-page report. He paused, giving her uninterrupted time to absorb what was on the printed page.

When her eyes raised, he quizzed, "Were you aware the program required participation of the child *and his or her parent*?"

"No. Nobody told me that. But—"

"Excuse me, Mrs. Woodward." His eyes homed in on a friendly, familiar face. Mr. Cromwell, the man he'd met at the seminar, was waving his hand. "Would you care to shed some light on this subject?"

Mr. Cromwell thumped the sheets in his hand. "You've summed it up in this report. The only thing I can add is that my son and I are talking to each other for the first time in months. The minute he became sixteen, my IQ dropped to the level of a blithering idiot. He knew everything; I knew nothing."

Heads nodded in empathy. Several chuckled at the honest confession they, too, could have been making.

"I'm not saying I've gotten any smarter, mind you, but at least we're talking to each other."

"Thank you, Mr. Cromwell." Damon grinned as he watched Tamara squirm in her seat. Was she uncomfortable with the praise, or the criticism? Her hand wasn't raised, asking for the floor, but Damon felt she should be given the opportunity to clear up any false beliefs. "Ms Smith, one of the teachers, is available for questions."

Tamara was halfway through the report when she heard Damon speak her name. Slowly she rose and turned in Mrs. Woodward's direction. She tried to smile, but couldn't. She was prepared to address the meeting about the reduction of faculty issue, but not the sex seminars. She'd have to wing it. Her knees trembled as every eye in the room focused on her.

"You aren't married, are you, Ms Smith?" Mrs. Woodward questioned, substantiating the point she'd made.

"No." Tamara shifted to one leg, tempted to revert to the "old Tamara" role and flaunt her attractiveness in such a manner as to say, "But that doesn't mean I don't have a lover, that I don't know about sex." Instead she leveled her blue eyes directly on the round face of Mrs. Woodward.

"The teenagers aren't married, either. And yet they are bombarded by television commercials, movies and peer pressure, all of which have strong sexual overtones. 'Come taste the forbidden apple. Try it, you'll like it.' The mixed signals, combined with curiosity, the desire to belong, and lack of information, lead to decision making based on ignorance."

Tamara didn't want to sound like a preacher in the pulpit, but in defense of the program, she had to establish a real need. She had to show Mrs. Woodward that married or unmarried she was fulfilling the needs of the students. Skepticism was still written on the older woman's face.

"Ignorance is not bliss. Ignorance is unplanned pregnancies." She locked her knees to steady herself, to be able to continue while observing several raised eyebrows. She could almost smell the stench from the old rumor about her reason for leaving Baylor City in the middle of her senior year. The pencil she held snapped under the pressure of her fingers. She raised her chin a fraction of an inch.

"The pilot program isn't going to keep them out of the back seats of cars. It isn't going to keep them from throwing wild parties when their parents leave town. Parents determine the moral attitudes of their children long before they reach high-school age. But the program does educate them as to the possible consequences of sexual involvement. Hopefully—" she glanced in Mr. Cromwell's direction "—we also open the doors of communication between the child and his parent. And once again, hopefully the teenagers benefit from accurate information."

Mrs. Woodward steadily held Tamara's gaze. "You ought to get married first," she muttered, turning back to the front of the room.

Taking her seat, Tamara wondered if the woman had referred to her unmarried state or the unmarried state of teenagers engaging in sex. Inwardly she grimaced. Mrs. Woodward hadn't backed off the issue; she'd muddled it. She wasn't going to allow herself to be confused with facts; Mrs. Woodward had made up her mind before she entered the building.

"We'll take your suggestion under advisement," Damon replied diplomatically. Damon glanced at the agenda, then toward the president. "Unless there are other questions or comments, I suggest we adjourn."

"I so move."

"I second."

Before Tamara had a chance to bring up the Reduction in Faculty policy, the gavel sounded, people began surrounding her. Her lips thinned. Didn't the board realize contract negotiations were closing in on them? Didn't they have any idea that the teachers were considering striking rather than see their ranks arbitrarily shrink? Threatening the board wasn't the answer. But neither was procrastination on their part.

While talking to the parents circling her, Tamara covertly watched Damon approach the tightly knit group. She had mixed feelings about him and his report.

"Yes, Mrs. Madison. Debbie mentioned your interest in the program. I'll look forward to your joining the group."

Tamara didn't have to turn her head to know who had lightly taken hold of her elbow. Involuntarily her arm jerked away as though scorched.

"Sorry," Damon apologized. "Didn't mean to scare you."

The glint in his eye belied his words. He knew the explosive chemistry between them ignited sparks. His own fingertips felt singed. Deliberately he recaptured the bend of her elbow.

The parents around them began dispersing as Damon silently walked her to the door. He kept his fingers lightly on her arm although he wanted to shake her sharply and demand a reason for her unwillingness to talk to him. They stepped into the darkness before he felt under control enough to be gracious.

Tamara caught a glimpse of color surging from beneath his pristine white collar. Anger, she guessed, remembering his accusations at the bowling lanes. Or was he embarrassed to be seen in public escorting her to her car? If that was the case, he shouldn't have joined the group.

"You didn't have to intervene on my behalf. I'm perfectly capable of defending the program and willing to do so." Her voice sounded strained to her own ears.

"Uh-huh," he replied noncommittally.

"And I know my way home, thank you very much," she stubbornly stated.

"Hmm." His hold tightened.

"I don't need a bodyguard!"

Damon grinned, finally in control, finally on the topic he wanted to discuss.

"Would you consider an apology?"

"Are you offering one?"

"Nope."

"Then there is nothing further to say, is there? That's why I didn't return your calls. We have nothing to discuss," she explained flippantly, wanting to ward off any questioning regarding the two-week-long silence on her part.

"We could have discussed the weather," he suggested inanely, once again making a grand effort to tamp back his temper. "The moon is beautiful tonight, isn't it? *Moonlight* becomes you."

Never slow on the uptake, Tamara caught his meaning and fought to keep from mischievously grinning. "Older ladies are partial to moonlight. The wrinkles don't show."

"Older ladies? Say my grandmother's age?"

"Mr. Foxx," she impishly chastised, "your grandmother wouldn't allow Father Time to etch her face."

Damon chuckled. "For once we agree on something. Care to celebrate over champagne?" Before she could refuse his invitation, he added, "I'd like some input from you on the RIF—Reduction in Faculty policy."

For some unknown reason, Tamara felt like celebrating. The leisurely walk to the car couldn't explain the way her heart pounded in her chest or her sudden shortness of breath. She glanced upward.

Maybe the moonlight was affecting her, making her slightly crazy.

"Okay." The sharp squeeze at her elbow relayed his surprise at her acceptance. "Business is often conducted over drinks, isn't it?"

"The school bell rang several hours ago, Tamara."

"And I have a stack of papers to grade. Maybe..."

"You do care about who's to be rehired and who's to be fired, don't you?"

He knew he was baiting her, but he couldn't, wouldn't, condemn himself to a month of silence until the next board meeting. And he wouldn't beg— not yet. Not until every other reasonable, pride-saving option had been tried.

"You know I do," Tamara whispered. "Follow me home, and we'll go in your car."

Victory left a bittersweet taste in his mouth. Dammit, he wanted her to show some enthusiasm. Her sacrificial-lamb attitude irked him.

He opened the car door for her and watched her roll down the window before she stuck the key in the ignition. "Tamara, I can't dangle the RIF policy as bait. It's against the law to falsely advertise." His voice lowered, barely audible as the engine came to life. "I want to be with you."

Unable to form a glib reply without betraying how much she wanted the same thing, she nodded and put the car into gear. She glanced in the rearview mirror. Damon had straightened, had stuck one hand in his pocket, but otherwise he hadn't moved an inch.

The light from the pole standard yards away cast a golden glow on his face.

As she turned the wheel, she remembered another time when she'd seen a similar look. Long, long ago—she couldn't have been more than seven or eight—she'd stolen across the tracks, while her mother worked, to walk down the shady, tree-lined street where Damon lived. She could almost hear the stick in her hand skittering across the wrought-iron fence, feel the wood vibrating with each noisy clank. The air was fragrant with summer's flowers. Atop a brick pillar at the end of a long circular driveway, she spied a redheaded kid watching her progress up the street.

Forever looking for a playmate, she'd called up to him, "Hey, Rusty, wanna go down to the creek for a swim?" Surely any kid with hair that color had to be nicknamed Rusty.

"Can't."

"How come? Your mom at work and you can't leave the yard?" She understood that. She'd spent many, many days stuck inside the boundaries of her small yard with nothing to do but watch the clouds. "I won't tell."

"Don't have a mom, but my dad would skin me alive for leaving the grounds without permission," he muttered.

Tamara shrugged one thin shoulder. "Spankin' don't hurt. Sure you don't want to come along?"

And that was when she saw the expression that recalled the memory as she drove toward Pickler Park.

The boy looked as though the hands he'd stuck in his back jeans pockets belonged to someone else, someone who held him back from what he really wanted to do. His face flushed. He jumped down from the pillar and kicked a loose stone on the concrete driveway.

"I don't wanna go."

Taking him at his word, she waved and tapped her way around the corner of his fence until she could see into his backyard. Her bright blue eyes widened. There, nestled under ancient oak trees, was the biggest pond she'd ever seen in her young life. No wonder Rusty didn't want to swim in the muddy creek.

Tamara grinned at the innocent recollection as she parked her car in front of her house. Rusty and Damon, she knew, were one and the same. But she also knew Damon Foxx had never had a nickname. Nicknames weren't dignified enough for the only child of Judge Foxx.

She unlocked the front door. The living room was dark, except for the flickering of colors on the television set. "Mom? You waiting up for me?"

Ginny Smith winced as she uncrossed her arthritic legs and lowered them from the ottoman to the floor. One gnarled hand turned the table-side lamp on.

"Tammy? Come in, child. I wasn't checking for holes in my eyelids." Her smile widened, making the lines beside her eyes crinkle upward at their standard family joke. Regardless of how loudly she snored, she wouldn't admit to sleeping in her favorite chair.

"I'm going out for a late snack, but I didn't want you to worry if you looked out and saw the car. You okay?"

"Fine. You don't have to go out for a snack. I'll fix you something."

"And miss the local news?" Tamara teased. "Next you'll be changing the channel when *Dallas* comes on."

"I can watch the news on the kitchen television, while I fix you something. Can't send you to bed hungry, now can I?"

Tamara crossed the room to hug her mother. The familiar smell of lavender and starch made her rub her cheek against her mother's cotton housedress. "Damon Foxx is taking me," she bubbled with excitement.

Her mother drew away from the hug. "Judge Foxx's boy?"

Tamara dropped a swift kiss on her mother's cheek. "Um-hmm."

"Don't set yourself up for failure," she warned, her pain evident in her voice as she slowly started to push herself out of the chair. "I don't want you hurt."

"Don't worry, mama. Damon Foxx isn't going to hurt me," she reassured her mother. "You watch the news and I'll be home before the late movie is over." The wary expression on her mother's face brought another quick hug from her daughter. "I'll be careful," she murmured.

They both heard the sharp knock at the front door.

"Remind me to tell you..." Ginny's knobby fingers patted her daughter's shoulder.

"Later, mama." Tamara straightened. She didn't want to keep Damon waiting, and more important, she didn't want him coming in. Her sweet mother seldom harped on anything, but getting mixed up with a boy from across the tracks had been a sermon she'd received time and time again during her teenage years. "Love you."

"Love you, too, darlin'. Do be careful."

The raps on the door sounded again, louder. Tamara quickly moved to answer it. "I'm ready. I wanted to tell my mother I was leaving."

She shut the door without inviting Damon in to meet her mother. A rude but necessary move.

Damon sensed that for some untold reason Tamara didn't want him inside her house. "You aren't a reverse snob, are you?"

"A what?"

He cupped her elbow with one hand and jammed his other hand into his pocket to jingle some loose coins. "Reverse snob. Holding my moneyed upbringing against me."

"Don't be silly," she prevaricated. "Don't you read the slick magazines? According to a very eminent psychologist, money won't make you happy, but it's way ahead of whatever is in second place."

"Psychologist or economist?" Damon lightly retorted.

"Actually," she teased, "I think it was an article on the front page of the want ads in the newspaper."

"Looking for another part-time job? Aside from the Guardian Angel service for the elderly?" He opened the car door and settled her inside. Her surprised glance, the rounded shape of her lovely mouth and the curious tilt of her head begged for a full explanation of how he'd gleaned those accurate facts. "You're dying of curiosity, aren't you?"

She chuckled as he shut the door and walked around the back of the car. Once he was inside the car, she turned toward him, curling her legs on the seat. "She gave you hell, didn't she?"

"You don't have to sound so cheerful about the prospect." Damon grinned. "Do you want the gory details of how a staid, respectable local businessman spouted off like a raving lunatic?"

"Tell all," she encouraged, blue eyes twinkling with contained mirth. "But I'm particularly interested in your grandmother's reaction."

Damon started the car and pulled away from the curb.

"First she marched into her bedroom and got her social calendar, which she flung at my feet. Second, she asked me if I'd care to give my official blessing to any future engagements." Damon paused, delighted by the musical laughter coming from Tamara. "Third, she flayed my hide with gentle curse words, such as, 'impudent, brash, idiotic, stuffed shirt.' Notice, not one four-letter word passed her lips." He chuckled as her laughter became loud enough for her to muffle it behind her fingers. "Don't spare me. Bring the roof down with laughter."

He turned down Main Street and headed for the highway leading to a nearby town outside the district boundaries, while Tamara wiped tears from her eyes. "And when she told me I should follow her example, I replied, 'There's fifty years age difference between you and a college lothario! I'd have to wait twenty years for the girl to be born before I could rob the cradle!'"

Tamara couldn't help herself; her giggles pealed from behind her hand. "You told your grandmother that? You're lucky she didn't..."

"Shoot me to put me out of my misery? No point. She said the men in the cemetery had a better love life than I do. She suggested I buy a little black book of my own and stay away from hers."

"Priceless," Tamara gasped. "Did you buy one?"

Damon reached into his coat pocket and pulled out an address book, then flipped on the interior light. "Read it out loud, please."

Fingers shaking from laughing so hard, she could barely get the small pages open. When she did, the laughter stopped. On each page there was one name: Tamara Smith.

Four

———

Don't look so stunned," Damon observed casually.

"I *am* stunned."

"Why? I'm obviously attracted to you. Persistence is a trait of every good real-estate developer. I don't give up easily."

The abrupt, serious turn in the conversation left Tamara momentarily speechless. Damon Foxx was persistent. A firm "no" in a schoolmarmish voice usually discouraged amorous advances. Tamara reached up and flicked off the overhead light. Her private thoughts were safer when Damon couldn't see the changing expressions on her face.

Did Damon see her silence as a challenge? Did he consider her like a prime piece of real estate? Did he think her refusal to enter into negotiations as a ploy to up the bid? Her heart sank. She wasn't a piece of property that could be sold to the highest bidder.

"Damon, I appreciate your support at the meeting tonight, but I can't get involved with a school-board member..." *Regardless of his effect on me.* To avoid looking at him, she turned her face toward the side window. The green sign marking the limits of the town east of Baylor City flickered by.

"You're running, hiding behind your job." He glanced at the digital clock on the dashboard. "It's ten-fifteen. We're outside the district boundaries and beyond the policy handbook. Do you want me to turn the car around?"

In all honesty, she didn't. But with her mother's warning ringing in her ears, with the broken hearts and divorces of many of her Pickler Park friends a constant reminder of the cost of becoming involved with a man from across the tracks, she didn't want to risk linking their names. But then again, his light-est touch set off fireworks in her bloodstream. Case histories, railroad tracks and warnings were feeble against the powerful yearning she felt.

"No."

He nodded, elated by her decision.

Her eyes studied his classic profile. His high brow, straight nose, sculpted lips were deliciously hand-some. Silently she admitted to being half in love with him. The crazy, wild half of her wanted to trail her fingers over the line of his smoothly shaven jaw. She wanted to taste his lips, to feel herself being drawn against his hard masculine frame. The feminine side of her wanted to kindle the fires burning between them rather than bank them the way the sane, logical part of her mind demanded.

Love was risky business.

Tamara avoided risk. Smart women did. They avoided emotional entanglement. Otherwise the consequences could be disastrously painful.

"It's after five. Forget the classroom. Concentrate on me," Damon encouraged, casting her a devilish grin.

"I'd be crazy if I did," she whispered, longing for the insane unpredictability of taking the risk. Fervently she wished she could throw caution to the winds and follow his lead. Once, just once, she'd like to indulge in her teenage fantasy of walking proud and tall beside Damon Foxx.

"Let's get crazy...together."

Damon isolated them by parking the car in the secluded darkness of the back of the lot beside the restaurant he'd chosen. He watched Tamara pensively bite her lower lip. Fear, he wondered. He gently threaded his fingers through her silky curtain of long blond hair.

Pressing the advantage he felt he'd gained, he promised, "I won't hurt you, Tamara." With infinite patience he closed the gap between them by sliding to her side of the car. He could see the mixture of fear and yearning in her eyes. "Don't be afraid of me."

She was scared, but not of Damon, only herself. Fully aware she could turn away and avoid his kiss, she remained motionless. His lips brushed against her forehead, her eyes, her cheeks. Anticipation of his claiming her lips clamored beneath each whisper of a caress.

"Damon?" A question or a plea—Tamara didn't know which. But for the moment, in the dark solitude of the car's interior, she wanted nothing more than to be thoroughly kissed. The consequences be damned.

She heard his soft groan, felt him tense as she framed his face between her hands. As though they turned back the hands of time, their lips met with the tentativeness of inexperience. They were both afraid of the kiss being too much, or worse, too little to satisfy the craving each of them felt.

Unsure of himself, of her response, Damon flicked the tip of his tongue across the bow of her lower lip. He longed to break down all the barriers between them. Massaging the tenseness beneath his fingers at the back of her neck, he yearned to eliminate the inhibitions she'd cultivated during the decade since he'd left town.

A passion Tamara hoarded, kept under lock and key, burst from deep within. Timidity quickly changed to assurance. She parted her lips, wanting to share the heat from the fires licking throughout her body. For a bare second Damon hesitated, then he took the sweet intimacy of her mouth as though he would starve without it. He shifted her across his lap, drawing her soft feminine curves against him. His hands erotically moved up and down her spine, urging her closer as his tongue probed deeper.

Their kisses strung together across timeless aeons until Damon was wild for more than kisses. He urgently wanted her. Here. Now. His face flushed as he sought control over his rampant desire. Once, twice, thrice, he boldly surged inside her mouth. His hand shook as he followed the gentle flare of her hip to her waist, to the swell of her breast. The small sounds he heard from the back of her throat made slowing their lovemaking impossible. Her nipple puckering beneath his thumb, budding in invitation to remove her tailored blouse, drove him to the brink of his self-control.

Slowly, unable to completely end the pleasurable sensations, he stopped as he'd begun—with hot, moist kisses over her entire face.

"Tamara, we've got to stop or I'll make love to you here, in an isolated parking lot, and love it." He felt as though his face was on fire. Control was close to being lost. His fingers slipped between the second and third buttons of her blouse. The round pearl button accommodated his desire by slipping out of its hole. Through her lacy bra he touched the tips of her breasts. His hand cupped the feminine fullness. "I need to kiss you here...and here."

Unable to resist, unable to think clearly under his mind-blowing ministrations, she arched against him. She trembled with desire as he parted her blouse, circling her nipple with his mouth, blowing his hot breath against her sensitive skin. A dewy moistness flowered from deep within. She didn't resist when he unclasped her last barrier of defense and nuzzled against her breasts. It felt good, better than good, wonderful. He pulled the taut bud between his lips; his tongue rasped against it.

"Make me stop, Tamara. Tell me no. But God, before you do, touch me," he begged, dragging her hand from his shoulder to below his waist. "Let me feel your touch. Then we've got to stop—got to stop," he moaned as her palm shyly pressed against him.

"Got to stop" echoed in her mind until it began to register. She didn't want to stop. She wanted more, not less. His mouth was suckling her soul from deep inside its prison. His hand painted sensuous pictures on her thigh. Never had she allowed any man to totally arouse her to the peak of her sensual nature.

He wanted; she loved. *Why not,* she questioned in the foggy passion surrounding her mind. She'd be bending the rules, but falling in love couldn't be bound by any rule book made by man.

As she silently made her irrevocable decision, Damon brought a sharp rein to his passion. He wasn't about to go any further in the front seat of the car. He knew when the heated air around them cooled, Tamara would construe it as common, cheap. Passionate seduction on his part would be the forerunner of equally passionate recrimination from her.

As though by mutual consent, their hands slowed. Damon clipped her lacy bra back in place and fastened each pearl button. He strove to control his breathing, but it came out in harsh rasps. He was doing the right thing, but damn, it had never been harder.

"Tamara, will you come to my ranch for the weekend?" he asked huskily. He refused to insult her by stating the obvious, that he wanted her. Instead he appealed to her logic. "We'll be far beyond the city limits and the town gossips. No school-board member; no faculty member. Just you and me."

She felt a thin film of perspiration on his forehead as she touched an unruly wave of his hair. "Earlier this evening I remembered a long time ago asking you to break the rules and go skinny-dipping with me." A smile tugged her lips upward.

"You called me Rusty. I remembered that incident...last week." The pause was filled with a quick kiss. "I wanted to go, but back then I was under my father's thumb. Will you go with me? There's a stream cutting through the ranch."

Tamara shivered. "The water will be freezing."

"I'll keep you warm."

"And safe?"

"I'll protect you."

Tamara shook her head, wondering if they were speaking in generalities or if he was speaking of the specific issue of birth control. "I'm capable of taking care of myself."

"Let me take care of you, even if it's only for the weekend. I want to. Monday morning you can return to Baylor City High and be strong and independent. Spend two days with me, please?"

Grinning at the thread of unspoken understanding between them, Tamara silently nodded, accepting his invitation. She heard his sigh of relief.

"Champagne is definitely in order. Come on, lady, I'm going to buy the biggest bottle of the best vintage champagne available."

And he did.

"To us," he toasted, clicking the rims of their glasses together.

"For the weekend," Tamara temporized. Tiny bubbles tickled her nose, making it itch. She sipped, then set the glass down to rub her nose.

"When your nose itches something good is going to happen," he teased, saying more with his eyes than what passed through his lips. "You won't change your mind, will you?"

When she promised not to change her mind, she hadn't foreseen the difficulty in keeping that promise. She changed her mind a dozen times during the week. At one point she considered taking the coward's way out by mailing him a contemporary greeting card with a cartoon chicken on the front, saying, "Sorry, Charlie."

She vacillated between glorious highs and depressing lows. Rationally she knew she was making the biggest mistake of her life. She was totally unsuitable for Damon Foxx, even for a brief affair. Like a bricklayer laying bricks, she placed one good reason after another in a row. By the time she'd built the equivalent of the Great Wall of China, she'd kick aside each reason, destroying the barrier. The simple truth of the matter was that she wanted to be with him.

Early Saturday afternoon she followed the map she'd found in her mailbox at work on Friday. The envelope had been marked "personal and confidential," but she guiltily scanned the faces of the office workers to see if anyone had read the contents. Why hadn't he called, given her directions over the phone? Deep down, she knew why. A call would have given her all the excuse she needed to bow out. She didn't call him for the same reason.

"Crazy," Tamara muttered as she turned in to the long winding, single-lane road leading to his ranch house. "Temporary insanity!"

Situated on a pine-tree-studded knoll, the two-story log cabin seemed to be a part of the land. It wasn't what she'd expected. Mentally she'd pictured a small duplicate of the Foxx house in town. But instead of a wide veranda with stately pillars she saw a small front porch with a wide swing. There was a charming masculine "homeyness" in the way the untrimmed floribunda roses climbed the trellis up the side of the house. They were a far cry from the formal rose garden in the backyard of Judge Foxx. Tamara could hardly wait to see the inside.

"Damon?" she shouted as she climbed out of the car. "Where are you?"

Her stomach twisted. Maybe he'd changed his mind about having a weekend guest. Maybe he finally realized what misfits they were. Maybe...

"Out here, Tamara—in the barn!"

"Some welcome," she muttered, disappointed. In her fleeting fantasies, she'd pictured Damon rushing off the front veranda, pulling her from her car and swinging her round and round, laughing, passionately stringing kisses along her arched neck. Tamara kicked the dirt with the pointed toe of her boot as she stuck her hand in the back of her jeans' pockets.

"Tamara!"

She followed the sound of his voice coming from behind the house. Dragging her feet, scuffing the sheen off her polished boots, she entered the barn. Her nose twitched as she smelled freshly cut hay and horses. A golden palomino whickered, inviting to be stroked.

"Back here, fourth stall," Damon instructed curtly.

He could have at least met me at the barn door, she derided. Miffed, she called, "If you're busy, I'll come back later."

The moment she entered the stall, saw his worried red-rimmed eyes and unshaven face, she knew the mare lying on the straw was in trouble. "Is the vet on his way?"

"Yeah, but I don't think he'll make it in time. He was tending to some sick cattle a hundred miles from here." His hands stroked the horse's flaxen mane.

"Heidi wasn't due for a week or two. I wanted everything to be right for us, so I gave Mac, the foreman, the weekend off."

Instinctively Tamara dropped to her knees to soothe the near-frantic horse. Dark brown pain-filled eyes blinked as she softly spoke to the pregnant animal. "It's okay, Heidi. Everything's okay. Calm down, love."

All four legs flayed as a contraction jolted her. Tamara comforted her with a low crooning voice. The forelegs of the horse stilled first, then the powerful back legs. She stroked the head of the animal, continuing to make reassuring sounds. As she watched the fear shining in the brown eyes, she was reminded of the panicked expression on her cousin's face when they took her into the operating room to perform an emergency caesarean.

"I'm glad you're here. I don't know how I'd have managed by myself," Damon confided.

Tamara kept her eyes on the horse, willing her pain to subside. "What can I do to help?"

"You're doing it. Keep her as calm as you can." Frustration edged his voice. "Dammit, I don't know enough about this!"

The realization that this could be the first birth Damon had ever witnessed paralyzed Tamara. They were both city born, city bred. It stood to reason he didn't know any more than she did. "Is this your first baby horse?"

"Foal," Damon corrected absently. "No. Mac and the vet delivered the last one."

"Did you watch?"

"I was at the office."

"Then I probably know more about this than you do," she blurted out, her voice raised an octave at the absurd possibility. The only thing she'd seen born was a litter of puppies. And when that happened, the mother took care of everything herself.

"From what I've read, and what I can feel, the foal seems to be in the right position," he reassured her, showing a basic knowledge of animal husbandry.

Tamara observed his capable hands as they cautiously, carefully skimmed over the mare's belly. "Then it's only a matter of time?"

Sitting back on his haunches, Damon plowed his hand through his hair. Wryly he conceded, "You're right. Women know more about birthing than men."

The second the words passed his lips, a memory jolted him. His head jerked up as he remembered details of the rumor he'd heard while he was away at college. *Tamara Smith had run away to Houston to have a baby.* How could he have forgotten? Had his mind purposely blotted out the stain on her reputation? Had he subconsciously chosen to remember only the unobtainable, virginal high-school girl? He wanted to ask if there was any truth in the rumor, but he couldn't.

His dark eyes shifted back to Heidi's struggle.

The thought of Tamara having another man's child unaccountably angered him. The thought of her being deserted by the father of the child further enraged him. The thought of her being alone and scared in a strange city tempered his anger with pity. Questions buzzed in his mind. What had happened to her baby? Was she forced into putting it up for adoption? The mare beneath his hands received more loving care than Tamara had. Lord, Lord, he'd be tempted to kill the man if they met face to face.

He needed time to sort through the way this piece of information affected their relationship.

"I've been at this since yesterday afternoon. Why don't you get the pot of coffee in the kitchen, make a couple of sandwiches and bring them out here? There doesn't seem to be much more we can do, but I want to keep an eye on her." He rubbed his eyes with the backs of his hands. "Hell of a poor way to welcome you to the ranch, huh?"

Tamara dusted the straw from her knees as she rose. "Don't apologize for something you couldn't control. I've told you before, I can take care of myself." She grinned impishly, hoping to erase the exhausted lines on his face with light humor. "The horse will do what comes naturally. Are you sure you'll be okay?"

Damon forced himself to grin. "Heidi is the one having the baby. I'm merely an adopted uncle!"

Smiling, Tamara left the stall. Her face froze as she remembered how callous her brother-in-law had been. While Martha was operated on, he hadn't even had the courtesy to pace in the waiting room. Why should he, he'd shouted over the telephone when Tamara called him from the hospital. He'd told her cousin he didn't want another kid, told her early in the pregnancy to get rid of it.

Tamara shook her head sadly. Married too young, unable to support herself and the four children she'd already had, Martha took the psychological abuse. Tamara hadn't been capable of offering much more than she'd given the horse...loving care. Tamara shivered, rubbing her arms. Women, her cousin being the prime example, managed to get themselves into the damnedest traps.

The back screen door creaked as she opened it. The smell of coffee filled the air. As she crossed to the refrigerator to investigate its contents, an unbidden thought crossed her mind: Damon Foxx would make a good father. He would cherish the woman who bore him children.

"Don't get yourself caught in any traps," she sternly warned herself. Her cousin hadn't expected the reaction she'd gotten from her husband, either. But Tamara had witnessed the mental cruelty heaped on Martha and covered her ears to block the bellow of his verbal abuse. She'd watched both of them sign the necessary papers to put the baby up for adoption. "Uh-uh. Not me! I know how to avoid those situations!"

She pulled a package of bacon out of the refrigerator. Damon needed something hot in his stomach, she decided, ignoring the half-empty package of cold cuts. Setting the meat on the stove top, she opened cabinet after cabinet searching for a frying pan. Finally she pulled out the drawer at the bottom of the ancient stove and extracted an iron skillet. As she searched for kitchen matches to light the gas stove, she hoped Damon wouldn't starve to death before she managed to fix the simplest of sandwiches.

More than a half an hour later, Tamara rushed across the backyard carrying a thermos, sandwiches, celery sticks and apples in a picnic basket she'd found stashed in the walk-in pantry.

"Tamara! I was just about to come and get you! Look!" Damon hustled her down toward the stall. "It's a girl!"

Tamara squealed in delight, dropping the basket on the bales of hay near the stall. Heidi was standing, licking, and encouraging her foal to rise. Tamara caught her breath as the copper-colored filly propped up her front legs, then seemed to heave herself onto her shaky, spindly legs.

"You should have called me when it happened."

"I did! I raced back and forth from the stall to the doorway. God, can you believe it? I delivered a baby!" Pride radiated from him as he lifted Tamara off her feet and swung her around.

"Filly!" she laughingly corrected, hugging him fiercely, as proud of him as he was of himself. "You're terrific, Mr. Foxx."

Damon grinned boyishly, crushing her against his chest, and crowed, "Yeah! I know!" Deep laughter rumbled from his chest.

"Put me down, and I'll feed the filly's proud uncle." As her feet touched the ground, she twirled to the stall to get one more peek at the mare and filly. The newborn was nuzzling the mare's belly. "Uh-oh."

Tamara instinctively knew what the filly was searching for. She entered the stall. Heidi nickered protectively.

In the same soothing voice the horse recognized, she gently spoke as she guided the velvet soft nose of the newborn to its mother. The filly inhaled, searching for a scent. Tamara milked a few drops into her hand, smiling when the filly began to suckle.

Damon watched. Moisture glistened in the corners of his tender brown eyes. For a woman who'd never been around horses, she instinctively knew what to do. But was it instinct, he wondered. Or did she have firsthand experience in taking care of a newborn? His heart seemed to swell in his chest as he leaned against the stall post. He wiped the unmanly tears from his eyes with his sleeve. They'd shared something wonderful.

And he knew. Deep inside, he knew he was falling in love with Tamara Smith. This tender, protective feeling, coupled with his strong desire to claim her as his own, had to be love. A lopsided smile twisted one side of his mouth upward. He'd fallen in love with the grown-up version of the little urchin who had tempted him years ago to break the rules.

"Want to eat here or in the kitchen?" Tamara asked, breaking into his private thoughts.

Damon glanced at the picnic basket and suggested, "How about down by the stream? We'll have to ride there, so go get a jacket and I'll take care of everything here."

A slow, meaningful smile passed between the two of them. Damon leaned down and brushed his lips softly against hers. "Be a good girl and scat; I'm hungry."

"I'm always a good girl," she quipped, provocatively exaggerating the sway of her feminine hips.

"I know better. That curl you had in the middle of your forehead when you were a kid was a dead giveaway. You were naughty, naughty, naughty!" he teased, admiring the way her jeans hugged her bottom. His voice lowered to a husky pitch as he added, "But, oh, so nice!"

Five

———

Where's the Bronco?" Bounding down the back steps, she shoved her arms into a lightweight jacket.

Damon led a palomino from the barn, fully saddled. "There aren't any roads leading to where we're going."

Grinning, Tamara shook her head. "I can drive a gas hog but not a horse. Rich city kids take horseback riding lessons, not—"

"Nothing to riding a gentle horse," Damon interrupted. "Any one who fearlessly faces those cowboys on the school board isn't going to balk at riding Goldie."

Hands on her hips, Tamara dug her heels into the dusty ground. "I'd rather go *in* the Bronco than *on* a bronco."

"Every Texan rides. It's an inherited trait. Where's your Texas patriotism?" His dark eyes glimmered with mirth at her obstinate pose. Appealing to her state pride wasn't working.

"I'm not about to get up on top of that four-legged high rise. I'd rather straddle the Empire State Building. At least it just sways."

"You came into Heidi's stall when her legs were thrashing, and you weren't scared. Come on, honey," he cajoled, "you're too courageous to let Goldie frighten you." He dropped the reins and strode to Tamara's side, chuckling.

"Damon, there's a big difference between helping an animal in trouble, one who needs me, and climbing on Goldie," she argued stubbornly. Goldie whickered, pawing one front hoof impatiently. "See? She's practicing. Getting ready to pound my bones into the dust."

Laughing, he firmly took her hand and led her to the horse. "Little five-year-olds have ridden Goldie. She isn't going to buck you off."

Glancing from Damon to Goldie to the hand-tooled saddle, Tamara stroked the near-white mane. "Will my school hospitalization cover me?" she teased, grinning.

"Yep." Damon cupped his hands. "Grab hold of the horn and I'll give you a boost."

"What about the reins?"

"She's trained not to move when the reins are on the ground."

Tamara bent her leg, placing her booted foot into his hands as she grabbed for the horn on the saddle. For one dizzy moment she thought Damon's boost was going to pitch her right over the side of Goldie, but she landed squarely in the saddle. Damon, as usual, knew what he was doing.

After placing her foot in the stirrup, he handed her the reins. "To turn right, move the reins to the right, and vice versa to go left. To make her walk, gently squeeze your legs."

Decidedly uncomfortable about her lack of control over the thousand-pound horse, she shifted on the saddle. His hand on her calf kept her from dismounting. "No steering wheel? No handle bars? I'm not wild about this idea, Damon. Why don't we double up on the same horse? Then I'll have something to hang on to?"

The thought of having her clinging to him held great appeal. "Okay. Scoot in back of the saddle. I'll get the basket."

Damon mounted, swinging his leg over the horse's neck and settling into the stirrups. His stomach muscles contracted when Tamara slid her arms around his waist. She snuggled against his back until she felt secure.

"Much better," she sighed, content to let Damon manage the horse.

Grinning at her absolute faith in him, he made a clicking noise and nudged Goldie with his knees. The horse slowly ambled forward in response to the rider's command. "Don't go to sleep back there."

"Oh, I won't. I'm about to grab the carrot you dangled in front of me to get me out here."

"The RIF policy?" He wondered what was responsible for his benevolent frame of mind. Was it Tamara's arms wrapped around him or just his lack of sleep? He lazily turned his head to nuzzle her ear. "Shoot, ma'am. I reckon I owe ya fer helpin' me with the mare. Ask away."

His playful caress momentarily distracted her. "Damon, be serious!" she reprimanded in what she hoped was her best schoolmarmish voice.

"Am I a breath away from getting a detention?" he teased, softly blowing in the vicinity of her ear. "Be warned, honey. I wouldn't mind staying after school with you."

"Does there have to be a cut in staff?" she asked, tempted to be led into a romantic verbal exchange, but resolved to grab the "carrot."

Sighing dramatically at her unwillingness to forget about business, he cleared his throat, unaware his father made the same sound before sentencing a convicted criminal. "Yes. Reduced enrollment means less state funding coming into the district's coffers."

"But, Damon, can't there be cuts elsewhere? For the first time in years the number of students in the classroom allows effective teaching to take place. Cut the staff and we'll have over thirty students each hour to teach. That reduces my effectiveness to the level of my being a glorified baby-sitter."

"The reports I've read state the teacher-pupil ratio is one to twenty."

Tamara snorted. "Statistics! When those figures are made up the entire administrative staff is figured in. I don't have one class with fewer than twenty-five students."

Spreading her fingers, she caressed the wide bones of his rib cage. One by one, she rippled her hands over them. By the time she reached his stomach, it was tight as a drum. She circled the dimple in his shirt above his wide belt buckle.

"Unfair practices," Damon huskily quipped.

Tamara shifted her shoulders away from his back as she stilled her questing fingers. "Better?" she teased.

"Terrible," Damon growled. "I'm pro practical education, remember? Continue with your 'hands-on' experiment."

Perfectly attuned to the gentle swaying of Goldie's placid gait, she withdrew her hands from around his waist to investigate the feel of his shoulders. Damon wasn't musclebound, but there wasn't a spare inch of flesh on his large frame. She trailed her hands over his shoulders, massaging the hollow of his back to remove the tense muscles knotted at the base of his neck.

"If cutting back on the staff is necessary, which I don't believe is true, who goes first? The new teachers?"

"Probably. Corporations make cuts based on seniority."

"The oldest teachers aren't necessarily the best teachers," she pointed out, thinking of Melissa. The bottom half of the professional ranks were filled with teachers from Pickler Park who'd struggled every step of the way to get certified. "Cut the young teachers, and you're back to letting the affluent teachers who don't really need the money remain on staff."

"Last hired, first fired seems the fairest way to do things. Ouch!" Her fingers bit into the flesh in the V of his collarbone.

"Sorry," she mumbled. She was far more sorry for those teachers losing their jobs, who would have to move away from their homes, than she was for inflicting a minor amount of pain to his shoulders.

"See that barbed-wire fence over there?" He pointed in the direction he wanted her to look. "It's exactly seventy-nine miles from the city limits."

"Is that a none-too-gentle hint to drop the subject?"

Damon nodded. "My subtle hint is about as gentle as your pinchy fingers. It's time to change the subject before I'm black and blue." He inhaled deeply as her arms wound around him. "I've thought about moving out here in a year or so."

"It's beautiful country," she conceded, wanting to probe further about the RIF policy, but knowing Damon had referred to the barbed wire as a clear-cut boundary between the city and where they were.

"Would you like to live this far from town?" he quizzed, changing the reins to the hand the picnic basket was in and resting his free hand on her knee.

Her knee pressed into Goldie's side. The horse responded by changing from the lazy walk to a brisk trot. Tamara clung tighter as she bounced from side to side. "Whoa!" she squeaked.

Tossing his head back, Damon laughed, continuing to leave the reins slack. "Want to go faster?"

"No," she gulped, squeezing her eyes shut.

Damon bumped the bit in the horse's mouth. Immediately Goldie slowed to her slow, rolling gait. "You'd learn to love it out here. Open your eyes and look around. We're five miles from the nearest house. The air is clear and clean. The pasture is knee deep in grass. And there are enough pine trees to build additions onto the house."

"You sound like a realtor making a sales pitch," she replied when she caught her breath. His fingers traced the double stitching on the outside of her jeans. Only the saddle kept her from moving closer, allowing his hands a wider range.

"I am a realtor." His thumb followed the narrow white line of the pressed crease.

"I guess I think of you spending all your time poring over the policy book, memorizing the rules," she teased, bumping the brim of his hat until it fell over his eyes.

He removed his hat and wiped a thin sheen of perspiration from his forehead. The weather had nothing to do with the gesture. He replaced his hat, wondering how long he could torture himself with the weight of her breasts jiggling up and down his spine.

Goldie stopped at the closed fence gate.

"Forget the school and the rules. This weekend there's only you and me. Hang on to the basket while I get the fence gate."

As Damon leaned over to unhook the loop of wire holding the gate to the post, Tamara got her first unrestricted view of what was ahead of them. They were about to enter a thicket. The road ended at the gate. A narrow path led the way into the dense bull pines. Damon maneuvered Goldie through the gate, turning her so he could shut the gate.

Before heading down the path, he turned, wrapped his arm around Tamara and swung her around to the front of the saddle. A boyish grin creased his lips, and his brown eyes glittered with accomplishment.

"Thought you might be tired of talking to the back of my head. Put your leg around the horn and your arm around my neck." Tamara mirrored his smile as she adjusted to the new position. "Comfortable?"

"Almost," she hummed, her blue eyes twinkling. "Take the basket." She linked her other arm around his shoulders. She squirmed against him, the underside of her leg sensuously rubbing against his upper thigh.

Damon inwardly groaned. "A cowboy always rode with his woman in front of him. It's a wonder they ever got anywhere."

"Maybe that's why history depicts them as the strong, silent type."

His reddish eyebrow raised. "Meaning?" he asked, willing to fall into her good natured trap.

"They chewed their tongues off trying to keep themselves under control."

Her open smile, the teasing light in her eyes, charmed him. Damon felt the heat rising from beneath his collar, spreading across his jawline. The ever-present desire he curbed came dangerously close to erupting.

Tamara fluttered her fingers over the same path. "Your thin skin betrays you, doesn't it? I've noticed when you're exercising iron-fisted control that your skin flushes." She shadowed the path along the strong column of his throat with her fingertips. "A very endearing trait. I'm curious to see what happens when you can't restrain yourself."

"Sweetheart, beware of the shackles of restraint being shed," he huskily warned. "I can think of two occasions when you nearly found out."

"At the bowling lanes?"

He nibbled her earlobe. "And in the car."

Tamara felt her heart quicken at the memory. "You're tired, remember?"

"Never *that* tired. You didn't answer the question I asked earlier. How would you feel about living out here?"

"With you?"

"With me."

She didn't know how to answer, so she took the easy way out. "You'd have to resign from the board. Would you resign?"

Damon hadn't thought of the election restriction. A board member was required to live in the school district. He hadn't thought of anything other than pressing Tamara into a commitment for more than one night.

"My term will be over in a few months."

Laughing, Tamara placed one hand on his face. "You could move in with my mother and myself," she teased, then, imitating a realtor giving the big sales pitch, she added, "The house is freshly decorated. The view of the railroad track is unrestricted. At midnight you can hear the lonesome wail of Engine 409 echoing down the tracks."

Damon appeared to be thoughtfully listening to her spiel, when in actuality he was concentrating on the rhythmic thrust of his hips against her. The innocent blue sparkle of her eyes told him she wasn't unaware of the effect the unintentional strokes were having on him.

"Okay," he answered in a distracted tone. "I accept."

"Accept? Accept what?"

"Your offer to share your house," he replied straightfaced. He thoroughly enjoyed the baffled pout of her lips.

"Now wait a minute. I was kidding."

"I wasn't."

"You can't move in with me," she contradicted, flustered by his casual acceptance.

"Why not? You asked; I accepted." Having decided to stop short of his originally planned destination, Damon swung his leg over the back of the horse and dismounted. He held his arms up to help Tamara.

She shook her head vehemently as he slowly lowered her down the length of his muscular body. His arms wrapped around her waist and stopped her downward motion when her face was level with his. "Kiss me, then say no...if you can."

His mouth slanted, closing over hers. The same thrill she felt when locked in his arms inside the car invaded her, making her cling limply against him. She couldn't fight, couldn't say no with his lips enticing her. Her mind whirled. In her wildest fantasy, she couldn't visualize Damon sharing her house. She had to refuse.

"No," she mumbled, her lips parting, giving him access to their honeyed recesses. Ever so sweetly, he filled her mouth as completely as he'd filled her thoughts during the past week. How could two people who fitted together so beautifully be so totally wrong for each other, she wondered then, and she wondered now. "No."

He brushed the curtain of blond hair away from her face. His lips caressed the lines marring her brow. Was she refusing because of the memories her care for Heidi had awakened? Did she realize he didn't care about her past? Without argument, he carefully lowered her until her feet touched the ground. He loosened the girth on Goldie as he watched her pick up the basket, kneel and begin spreading the contents on the grassy glade.

Tamara was confused. He couldn't be serious about moving in with her, could he? The idea would be laughable, if it weren't so heartwrenching. A wry grin drew her lips upward. She visualized Damon Foxx moving in the front door, and her mother moving out the back door. The preposterous scene would have the neighbors sitting on their front porches, clutching their sides with laughter. She pictured a cartoon figure of Judge Foxx arriving on a trusty white charger, frantically waving a moral-conduct book.

She blinked, obliterating the absurd picture from her mind. Sitting back on her heels, she raised her eyes. Damon had remained standing beside Goldie, one arm resting on the saddle, the other on his hip. How easy it would have been to say, "Yes, Damon, let's live together." But she couldn't take the easy road. There were too many roadblocks. The easy road led to a dead end.

"Come and eat."

Damon wiped his damp palms on his thighs. Determined to clear the air, determined to keep a tight rein on his desire, he folded his long legs and sank to the ground Indian-style.

"Why?"

Like the concerned parent at the board meeting, Tamara had made up her mind. She didn't want to be confused with logic or facts.

"Because..." she floundered. The list of reasons was too lengthy for an afternoon discussion. They'd be there all night!

The passionate side of her nature longed to change her no to a fervent yes. But the sane, practical side recoiled at the idea. She'd just be another girl shacking up with the son of one of the founding fathers of Baylor City, Texas.

"Of your own free will, you came to me this weekend, and I'm staking a claim." Damon picked up a piece of celery stuffed with pimento cheese and nibbled on it as though they were discussing the weather.

"I'm not a piece of property you can homestead!" she sputtered. She grabbed half a sandwich and bit into it.

Damon tunneled into the cream cheese with the tip of his tongue. "No, but you're going to be mine."

"Only your arrogance exceeds your..."

"Libido?" Damon chuckled.

"Common sense," she finished, taking another bite. "I'm here for the night. Don't expect more, then you won't be disappointed."

Picking up the other half of the sandwich, Damon devoured it. The prospect of convincing Tamara how wrong she was didn't diminish his appetite. "You're not eating," he observed when she put her half of the sandwich down on a paper plate.

"I've lost my appetite."

Damon picked up her half, turned it so his lips covered the dainty bite she'd taken and bit down. Tamara felt as though he'd swallowed her whole. His eyes never left her face. He seemed to be gathering strength for the next verbal battle with each bite he took.

Minutes later, his appetite for food assuaged, he edged backward until he leaned up against the trunk of a pine. Stretching his long, jeans-clad legs out, crossing his ankles, he winked lazily, crooking his finger toward her. "Come here."

She ignored his beckoning hand. Her eyes fastened on the patterns of sunlight dancing on Goldie's golden coat. "I'd rather talk."

Following the direction of her pensive eyes, he chuckled, then said, "You'd rather run."

"I've told you, I don't run from problems."

"I won't let you run—from your problems or from me." Damon leaned his head back onto his interlaced fingers. His hat, nudged from the back, tipped over his brow.

Tamara picked up an apple and bit into it, thoughtfully munching on the tart skin. She hadn't expected Damon to want more than one night. She'd counted on that. Her final decision to get in her car and drive to the ranch was based on her belief that once the explosive sexual attraction Damon felt for her had run its course, they could resume their lives in a sane fashion. Dammit, from the beginning he'd known what the rules were in their relationship. Deciding he must have been teasing all along, she cast him a cheeky grin.

"You'd have croaked if I'd agreed to letting you move in, wouldn't you?"

"Nope. I'll admit I'd rather have you move to my house." He grinned. "Without your mother."

She chuckled. "Doesn't this show you how hypocritical the policy handbook is? I can't consume alcoholic beverages within the city limits, but I could live with you."

Damon, with a swiftness belying his relaxed pose, bent forward and snagged her wrist, pulling her against his chest. "You can drink at my house. You just can't drink in public. We can't have our faculty staggering up and down Main Street, now can we?"

Laughing, she braced one hand against his chest. "You are not moving into my house, and I'm not moving into yours."

"I didn't expect you to make the offer to begin with," he teased, brushing his finger over the bridge of her nose. "But once you made the offer, I felt obligated to accept your hospitality."

Tweaking the copper-colored hair at the V of his collar, she purred against his neck, "You're a clever scoundrel, Damon Foxx."

"Perhaps. I'm also patient, persevering and persistent. I'll settle for less, but I won't allow you to use the handbook as a bolster in our bed."

"Listen carefully, and watch my lips." She spoke slowly, exaggerating each syllable. "I will not be drawn into a full-scale affair with you or anyone.

Not with the entire faculty, the entire school board—
hell, the entire town—looking on. Got it?''

Sliding his hand over the gentle curve of her hip,
he lightly kissed her sensitive temple. ''Got it.''

She groaned at the lack of sincerity she heard in his
voice. The light pressure of his fingers pushing her
into the cradle of his pelvis confirmed her suspicion.
The three qualities he used to describe himself were
accurate. He was gently patient, unswervingly persevering and the essence of persistence.

The reins of contol Damon held began to slip.
Back in the barn, while she was fixing something to
eat, he'd decided to show her how much he respected her by ignoring his masculine desire. If he
could behave himself, be a gentleman in the purist
sense of the word, she'd know she could trust him.
And if he could gain her trust, she'd open up to him.
She'd learn to love him. In the barn, this plan of action seemed sound. But with Tamara this close, her
fresh scent so appealing, he felt sorely pressed not to
give in to his desire.

''What would you like to do this afternoon?'' he
asked, forbidding himself to let his mind wander in
a dangerous direction.

''You're exhausted from staying up all night with
Heidi.'' Her fingers walked up the pearly buttons on
the front of his shirt. ''You don't have to be the per-
fect host with me. Why don't we go back to the
house? You can take a nap.''

''Hmm. What are you going to be doing while I'm
sleeping?''

"I have my lesson-plan book in the car." Her blue eyes were round and innocent as she flirted outrageously. She slipped two fingers between his second and third button. "Or—" her voice lowered to a sultry pitch "—I could take a nap myself."

Damon closed his eyes. The thought of them *napping* together sent his thoughts racing full gallop down the path he'd tried to avoid. He couldn't think of an alternative plan half as pleasant. His jaw clenched with determination.

"Do you play chess?"

Tamara knew he was teasing again. "Nope."

"Checkers?"

"Nope."

"Parchesi?"

"Nope." The game she had in mind wasn't found in a toy store. Snuggling closer, she plucked at his chest hair. His deferment of the inevitable had a special charm. He obviously wasn't going to rush his fences.

"There's a football game on television we could watch."

Tamara yawned, stretching sensuously against him.

Damon felt his good intentions crumbling like a cardboard house in a windstorm. Without intending to, he found his hands drawing her against his chest. Disgusted with himself, his lack of self-control, he straightened, pushed his hat back and stood up. He kept his back to Tamara, hiding his primitive reaction to her closeness by tucking his shirttail into his pants.

Tamara reassessed their conversation. Apparently, since she refused to extend the length of time they would share, he'd changed his mind. He didn't want her, after all.

Her pride stung severely. Ashamed of herself, she scrambled to her feet and strode to Goldie's side.

"Decide to ride by yourself?" He moved to assist in cinching the girth. "Wait a minute."

"Don't move a muscle, Mr. Foxx. For the umpteenth time, I'm telling you I'm perfectly capable of taking care of myself."

"But—"

"After your superb tutelage on the way out here, I'll manage very nicely, thank you very much!" The hurt she'd felt over his rejection quickly changed to anger. Her stubborn pride refused his polite offer of assistance. She wasn't going to meekly climb up behind Damon and ride back to the house. She'd ride, and he could damned well walk!

Damon grinned. Given the choice, he preferred to calm her ruffled feathers than let himself be tempted beyond his control. He watched her struggle to raise her leg onto her waist to reach the stirrup. Her skin-tight jeans made the task impossible.

"You need to—"

"Keep your advice to yourself," she huffed, grabbing the reins and leading Goldie to a stump. She flung a triumphant smile at Damon when she settled into the saddle.

"Be careful," Damon cautioned. "You're in for a fall."

"Not likely." Her clipped words were barely spoken through her clenched teeth when the saddle began slipping to the side.

Damon grabbed the reins. Goldie snickered and stopped. "Sweetheart, I ought to let you take your lumps." He nudged her leg aside and tightened the girth. "But I did promise not to hurt you, didn't I?"

Tamara wanted to dig the horse in the sides and gallop off, but she knew she'd totally disgrace herself by winding up flat on her face, eating dust. "The reins, please," she demanded haughtily.

"Brrrrr!" Damon shivered. "You asked me what happens when I lose control. What happens when the tempestuous Tamara Smith of ten years ago runs out of ice?"

She snatched the reins out of his loose grasp and leaned down. Tempted to wipe the lopsided smile off his face with the palm of her hand, she substituted a verbal swipe. "Put a fan behind Goldie's tail and you'll find out."

Her fear of his recriminations outweighed her fear of horses. She clicked her tongue and squeezed her knees.

Six

Tamara bounced in the saddle, clinging to the horn, while Damon burst into laughter. What the hell did he mean by goading her into a response diametrically opposed to the way she'd carefully trained herself into behaving? He'd be the first one on the board to vote for her dismissal if she gave rein to her temper in the classroom!

"You're running again!" His taunt echoed through the cathedral branches of the pines overhead.

She whipped around in the saddle to respond. Her teeth jarred together as Goldie reacted to her jerking the reins. The horse spun around on her back legs. Off balance, teetering, Tamara clenched her legs together and sawed back on the reins. Confused by the simultaneous, conflicting commands to both halt and charge forward, Goldie reared. The front hoofs barely left the ground before Tamara pitched sideways. The needle-strewn ground seemed to swirl around her. She heard a high-pitched scream, felt herself falling as Goldie jerked in the opposite direction. Arms flung wide, legs splayed, she bellyflopped onto the ground. Air whooshed from her lungs.

Her scream had the same effect on Damon as a blank being fired at a track event. Ashamed of himself for egging her into proving she was independently capable, scared she'd hurt herself, he plunged through the bramble instead of following the natural curve of the path. Blackberry thorns tore at his jeans. A low branch knocked his hat off. But Damon didn't notice.

His promise returned to haunt him. *I won't hurt you. I won't hurt you. I won't hurt you.* Legs churning, he swiftly covered the distance between them.

Tamara struggled to suck air into her burning, oxygen-starved lungs. Her heart seemed to be lodged in her throat, blocking the passageway. She swallowed. The taste of pine resin and red clay exploded on her taste buds. Tears streamed down her face.

"Tamara! My God! Tamara!" Panic was apparent in Damon's voice. He knelt beside her, turning her into his arms, swiping the reddish dirt and pine needles from her precious face. "Are you hurt?"

Her eyes widened at the fear written on his face. "No," she sputtered, her chest heaving.

"Are you sure?" His hand trembled as it quickly brushed over her arms, her legs, seeking any evidence of broken bones.

"Just had the wind knocked out of me," she croaked, her throat raw and dry.

When she tried to sit up, Damon crushed her to his chest, slowly rocking her back and forth. "I'm sorry, Tamara. I shouldn't have..."

"Don't apologize." Taking a flying leap from Goldie's back was worth the small price if Damon continued to hold her, stroke her. She curled her arm around his hunched shoulders. "My fault."

"The hell it was. I knew you didn't know how to ride. I should have stopped you."

Her breathing and her sense of humor slowly returned. "You couldn't have. I'm a mite stubborn when I'm mad."

"That doesn't excuse my goading you." He leaned her back in the cradle of his arms. The fleshy pad of his thumb erased the smudge from her high cheekbones. "Are you sure you aren't hurt?"

Tamara shakily grinned. "The expression 'easy as falling off a horse' must be the epitome of sarcasm." Her grin spread wider. "That first step was a doozy."

Her smile was infectious. Damon found himself grinning back at her, but he vividly remembered how scared he'd been. Mentally he still cursed himself for putting her in danger.

"Rest a minute. I'll catch Goldie, and we'll go back to the house."

"You couldn't pay me enough to climb back on that wild hellion," she protested, her hand clutching the back of his neck.

Damon, wanting to give his word that he'd take care of her but knowing she'd never believe him, raked his hand through her hair to remove the bits of forest debris.

"I'll walk." Uncertain she'd be able to stand on her rubbery legs, her bravado sounded faint. "I can do it."

Damon shook his head. With her stubborn streak, she'd crawl if necessary. Convincing Tamara to trust him, put herself faithfully into his hands, would be close to impossible. But what choice did he have?

"I'll hold you," he reassured her. He glanced at Goldie, grazing the sparse growth beside the path. "I can't imagine why Goldie acted up."

"My jerking on the reins, screaming and digging my heels in her sides must have frightened her," she confessed, realizing she'd done everything wrong.

"She appears to have calmed down."

His own reactions to having Tamara locked in his arms was anything but calm. Her softness melted against the hard contours of his body. His hand, which innocently rested at the base of her slender throat, began to pulsate heat, matching the vulnerable throb of the vein beneath his fingers. His dark eyes lowered to the full swell of her breasts lying beneath his forearm. Just looking at her made his mouth water.

Yes, there was a red smudge on the tip of her nose. Yes, her sleeve was ripped at the shoulder. And yes, her jeans were covered with a thin film of dust. But Damon didn't notice.

His eyes were drawn to the enticing moisture glossing her lips after she'd nervously licked them. The fragrance of a wild-flower-bouquet perfume coming from the valley between her breasts lured him. His ears filled with the roaring of his own hot blood pounding a primitive message to his brain.

What the hell was wrong with him? The woman he'd sworn to protect had taken a violent fall from his trusty horse, and he wanted to throw her into shock by ripping her clothes off and making love to her. What had happened to the solemn vow he'd made in the barn? For long seconds, he purged his mind, his straining senses, of the effects she had on him.

Tamara observed the slow, creeping tide of control wash over his rigid jaw. Although he didn't move, she felt him withdraw. Whatever tempted him, he'd pushed aside. Just once, she mused, just once she wanted him to release his pent-up emotions. But, she silently concluded, whatever made him tighten the reins of control, he had to freely let go.

Decisively Damon crooked his arm beneath her knees, and stood up. His lips pressed together into a thin white line. His grim expression temporarily silenced any protest on her part.

"Damon, put me down. I can walk."

His tongue clicked on the dry roof of his mouth. "Come here, Goldie."

"Put me down! Dammit, you can't make me get back on that horse!"

Ignoring her adamant protest, Damon firmly hoisted her into the saddle, then swung up behind her. "Rest easy, honey. I'm not going to let anything hurt you."

Hours later, as she changed into the sleek, satin-textured, black negligee she'd packed, the impact of his words hit her squarely in the stomach. The entire afternoon and evening he'd been solicitous, kind and polite, which totally baffled her. At first she enjoyed being treated like a rare porcelain antique. But by nightfall, it palled. His chaste, brotherly kiss as he bid her goodnight left an empty feeling in the pit of her stomach.

"Is he rejecting me or saving me from himself?" she mouthed as the cloud of fabric settled around her ankles. Why did he think she agreed to drive out to the ranch? Dammit, he'd asked her right after practically seducing her in the restaurant parking lot. She didn't want to be saved!

Folding her empty arms over her chest, she tapped her bare foot impatiently on the hardwood floor. Come to think of it, she fumed, since they'd left the barn his entire demeanor, excluding one or two slips, had been that of a classic gentleman. He'd even held the chair for her when they sat down at the kitchen table to eat dinner. How absolutely absurd!

She paced noiselessly around the oval braided rug beside the bed. She heard the bedsprings creak on the other side of the wall separating them.

Frustrated by his lack of interest, she curled her fingers around her chin and tapped her lower lip with one finger. She squeezed her arm against her waist to contain herself. For two cents, she'd go over and pound on his door and ask him what the hell was going on. But his answer would be devastatingly simple: nothing. Absolutely nothing!

She stared balefully at the notched logs between them. What had he said earlier about not allowing the policy handbook to be a bolster in the bed between them? What about A Guide to Southern Gentleman's Hospitality, she thought derisively. How many rule books did he have stocked in his library?

"Thousands," she muttered discontentedly.

Again her mind skittered and bumped over what had taken place. She recalled the fiery lights in his dark eyes after he'd instigated her into responding like the "old tempestuous Tamara Smith."

An idea popped into her mind. She shook her head. Her shoulder-length hair swirled around her shoulders sensuously. He'd probably think she was some sort of a sex-starved lunatic if she followed her impulse.

"I couldn't," she whispered, a spark of defiance twinkling mischievously in her blue eyes. The first genuine smile of the evening curved her lips upward. "Yeah, I could."

Damon didn't have any qualms about sidestepping the unwritten rules when it came to who they were or where they came from. It didn't in the least bit bother him that she was employed by the district over which he presided as board member. Nor did he pursue the issue of her moonlighting once he'd found out she wasn't fixing up little old ladies.

Her smile parted her lips. She flicked her tongue across her painted fingernail.

There weren't any written or unwritten rules in any of his books as to how she could conduct herself when in this situation. A low husky chuckle bubbled through her lips.

"Damon?" she called softly. "Are you awake?"

"Is something wrong?"

Her head swiveled from the wall to the door. Strange, she thought, his voice seemed to be coming from the opposite side of the door. The log construction must affect the accoustics. "No. I can't sleep."

"Me either. Want to share a pot of hot chocolate?"

Tamara grinned. Unless he had icicles instead of good hot Texan blood running through his veins, he'd acquire a thirst for more than hot chocolate.

"Hot milk does make me sleepy," she agreed with provocative innocence.

Tamara crossed the room and opened her door. A good sign, she mused when she saw Damon in the hallway. He hadn't wasted any time getting there. "I'll fix it," she graciously offered.

The light streaming from inside the room accentuated the lovely curves beneath the sheer gown. Damon stood as though struck by lightning. His throat worked convulsively. He tugged a knot into the cloth belt of his thigh-length midnight-blue robe.

"Back to bed," he ordered gruffly.

He lowered his blazing eyes to the floor to avoid letting them slowly follow each delicious curve beneath her gown. Damon clenched his jaw. Five minutes alone in the kitchen, with both of them barely clothed, and his temperature would be high enough to boil milk in the palm of his hand.

"No," he abruptly refused. His hoarse, bullfrog voice sounded alien to his own ears. He heard a tiny gasp from the doorway. "You're probably suffering from delayed shock. You get back under the covers."

Was that why he'd changed the original plans, she wondered. He thought she was in shock? "I'm hail and hearty," she staunchly refuted. "I can make my own hot chocolate."

"You're going to catch pneumonia." His jaw ached from being held tensely. "Don't be stubborn. Get back into bed."

"Don't order me around," Tamara defied. She wasn't going to meekly retire under a bundle of quilts. "You go back to bed if you're worried about how cold it is out here."

He opened and closed his fist, raising his head to the ceiling, inhaling deeply. Cold? His entire body felt enveloped by flames.

His voice shook. "Tamara Smith, if you have the sense God gave a goose, you'll lock and barricade that door, climb under the blankets and cover your head. I'm warning you..."

Tamara grinned. "I can't hear you. Could you come a little closer? Or shout a bit louder?"

"Dammit! I'm trying to be a gentleman."

"You don't seem to be enjoying the role," she observed, rolling her tongue in her cheek. "Why did you invite me to the ranch? To watch you become an uncle? To break my neck bronco riding? To play solitaire while you took a nap?"

Drops of perspiration beaded on his forehead, his upper lip. He yanked another knot into his belt. "You know why I invited you here."

"I don't think I do," she softly replied, coaxing, "Forget the Code of Conduct book. Tell me."

Damon looped another knot into his belt. "I wanted—"

"Past tense?" She moved toward him.

Want...need...desire...crave! He shuddered. His vocal cords constricted. The seductive sway of her feminine hips mesmerized his dark, glowing eyes, leaving him speechless.

Tamara hesitated, then stopped when she felt the heat radiating from him. The darkness could no longer conceal the red flames licking a path from the gaping V of his robe to the roots of his hair. His hands, turned palm upward. They settled on her rib cage.

Damon battled with his good intentions.

For long, long moments their eyes clung to each other's. Her blue eyes beckoned him, tempted him. Unashamed of her boldness, she abandoned pride and stubbornness by stepping closer. Her heart clamored in her chest as she waited.

"Present and future tense," he whispered barely audibly.

A flood of ecstasy made her eyelids flutter shut. "Oh, Damon," she breathed, cupping his jaw as gently as his hand cupped the weight of her breast. The fleshy tips of her fingers fanned over his lips. The dewy moisture they removed eloquently told her how valiantly he'd fought to adhere to his principles.

His head bent to the hollow at the base of her throat. "I want you now more than I did a decade ago. You've become an obsession." A strangled laugh escaped his lips as he nipped love bites on her earlobe. The tip of his tongue circled the gold bead nestled in the lobe. "I remember when you had them pierced."

"The whole town was horrified."

"Oh, Tamara, how I wanted to kiss the pain away." As though they'd both stepped into a time warp, he curled his tongue to the back of her lobe, gently stroking away any residue of pain. "We'll make up for the time we've lost."

When the tip of his tongue circled, hot and wet, slowly flicking, dipping in and out, Tamara felt a shaft of pleasure jolt through her. Knees weak, she leaned heavily against him for support. Her arms circled the strong column of his neck; her hands buried themselves in the thick richness of his straight auburn hair.

He must have known she could barely stand. In one deft motion, he raised her into his arms and carried her down the short hallway, into his room. She was breathless, floating, eager. The sleekness of her gown clung to the rich velour of his robe. She realized the chance of either of them changing their minds was slim, but still she couldn't believe they were twined together.

His lips feverishly slanted over hers as he brushed the covers aside to accommodate both of them. They lay side by side, locked in a lovers' embrace. Their tongues parried, circling, advancing, retreating. She held nothing in reserve.

"Tamara, love, I've waited so long for you. I'm nearly out of control. Caught between wanting to savor your sweetness slowly and wanting to take you quickly, hard and fast." He crushed her against his chest; her breasts flattened against the lapels of his robe. "God, I want tonight to last forever."

He rolled to his back, taking her with him, settling her against his strong thighs. One hand eased a thin strap off her shoulder, while the other reached for the drawer in the bedside table. Tamara touched his sleeve. Her hair shimmered in the moonlight shining through the window.

"No. I've taken care of it." Her eyes burned brightly. She did practice what she taught. A woman who didn't take precautions risked more than her happiness. She risked her future, her fate. But she truly appreciated his protective gesture. "Thank you."

Both his hands settled on her shoulders. The soft fabric of her gown crumpled downward, leaving her breasts bare, kissed by the silver light. She heard Damon take a deep breath. His fingers followed the shadowed cleavage. His knees squeezed together. Ever so slowly, she felt herself slide against his legs. His robe parted from the waist down. The hard knots in his belt pressed against the softness of her stomach. As his thumbs circled the dusty pink aureoles of her breasts, she pushed aside the top part of his dressing gown. She echoed his movements. His nipple puckered between her thumb and forefinger. He groaned from deep in his chest.

"I want to taste you."

He rolled her to her back. Greedily his moist lips sipped one diamond-hard nipple, then the other. She arched against him. The heat of his mouth, the lightly abrasive stroking his tongue made, sent flames of desire coursing through her. She buried her hands in his thick hair. His teeth closed over her less gently, knowing a light touch wasn't what she wanted.

"Let me take your robe off," she requested, wanting the cloth barrier between them to magically disappear but knowing it wouldn't. A tremor ran through her hands as they untied one knot, then another, and another, until finally the belt was undone.

A wry grin on his face, Damon raised his head, his torso, and then took off his single garment. "Each knot represents the effort I made to control myself."

"Waste," she whispered, unable to speak as her eyes filled with him. Her arms circled his neck as he lowered himself, pushing her deep into the softness of the mattress. Her heavy-lidded eyes closed, relishing the feel of his muscular length.

"Never a waste...always an asset," he mumbled, silently hanging onto the last shreds of his self-control. Her hands sliding over the curve of his back and the narrowness of his waist, threatened to blow his resolve to make love to her slowly. Her sleek, slender leg sensuously caressed his. He squeezed his eyes shut until minor explosions burst behind the lids. "I meant to love you slowly, lazily. But I can't. Not the first time. I want you too badly. I'll be a gentleman next time."

Tamara didn't want temperance. Writhing beneath him, arching beneath his hand, she beckoned each bold touch, delighted in the spontaneous groans coming from the back of his throat. His hands swept from her breasts to her knees. Her nails dug into the hardness of his buttocks.

"Please, Damon..." she begged as his fingers sought and found the source of her inner heat. She pushed against the heel of his hand, rotating her hips. "Please."

He came to her with a boldness that sent pleasurable tremors through her. She met each thrust, her nails biting into the hard muscles of his back. Damon Foxx made love with the tenderness of this being the first time, and the confidence that it wouldn't be the last. Tamara matched his long, sure strokes. Her arms and legs wrapped around him as though the dizzying heights they climbed were perilous. Unexpectedly she felt him withdraw.

"Damon!"

"Shh, honey."

The heel of his hand rotated against the tight bud of her desire. His attempt to slow his ragged breath, to recompose himself, to regain control, made Tamara swipe his wrist away. "No!"

"I know what I'm doing..."

Tamara clenched her legs tighter, guiding him deeply inside her. Intimately locked, they each remained still. She wiped the thin line of perspiration from his upper lip with her thumb. "Would you want me to fake it?"

"God, no!" he whispered. "I just—"

"Just love me, Damon."

His mouth slanted over hers. Through her parted lips, his tongue echoed the thrusts of his hips. He loved her as he'd wanted to in his youth—wildly, passionately, without mentally following any guidelines from any how-to books.

She gasped his name as he raised her hips and buried himself in her with one final, ecstatic thrust.

The natural, unchecked ardor spiraled Tamara over the brink into unfettered rapture.

Long moments later, Tamara shifted beneath his weight. A blend of strong masculine smell and the remnant of this morning's after-shave cologne compelled her to rub her cheek against his chest. Damon smiled as he rolled both of them to their sides. His hand followed the sweet curves of her waist and hips.

"Sweet, sweet temptress," he crooned next to her ear.

Tamara sighed, contented, satiated, lazily stretching. "Would you have slept in the other room?" she asked, curious to know if his gentlemanly code could have kept them apart.

"Slept? No." A low chuckle rumbled from his throat. "Thank God you seduced me out of the room."

"Temptress? Seductress?" she questioned, not certain she liked the image he was painting.

Propping himself up on one elbow, he grinned that devilish, lopsided grin that made her heart beat faster. "You've tempted me the entire day."

"I tempted you in the hallway," she corrected, "but—"

His fingers sealed her lips from further denial. "Honey, just watching you walk sends my temperature gauge ten degrees upward. When you chew on your bottom lip, I'm tempted to kiss away whatever is worrying you. Your stroking the mare or helping the filly tempts me to hug you until I receive the same tender loving care. Not to mention having you melt against my back when we rode Goldie. I'd be embarrassed to tell you how many times I've been tempted to make you mine."

"Then why the buddy treatment this afternoon and all evening?"

Damon brushed his lips over hers. "Because—" he peppered a string of kisses along her jaw "—I didn't want you waking up in the morning asking me if I respected you?" he answered, half teasing, half serious.

Twisting several reddish-brown chest hairs together, she lightly tugged them. "Would you respect me more if I'd left you alone?"

His large hand covered her breast, worrying her beading nipple at the joint of his fingers. "No. I want you more than I've wanted any woman," he confessed sincerely.

"More than anyone from your own side of the tracks?"

"More than anyone in the whole damned country," he groaned as her hand moved from his shoulder to his hip. His lips fused over hers. His leg curled over her hip, cradling her against his pelvis.

Tamara realized he had confused want with respect. But for now, while her heart thrummed wildly, while the rules were being suspended, she didn't quibble over semantics. Between them, the primitive language of passion and desire was clearly understood.

Seven

———

Tamara snuggled deeply under the hand-stitched quilts. Her eyes gradually opened to see rays of early-morning sunlight dancing merrily on the cross-stitch bedding. For a moment she was disoriented. This wasn't her bed, her room. She rolled to the center of the double bed. Her hand touched the imprint in the pillow next to hers. Cold. Where was Damon? She sat up and crossed her legs.

Daylight restored her sanity. Mixed emotions began warring inside her head. A rosy blush suffused her cheeks. *My God,* she thought. *What did I do last night?* Had she really seduced Damon Foxx, vice president of the Baylor City School Board?

Recalling the pique she'd felt when given a platonic peck on the cheek, she silently acknowledged that she couldn't accuse Damon of dragging her into his bedroom and ravishing her. She had been the one who had taken matters firmly into her own hands. What the hell was the matter with her? For years she'd led an exemplary, chaste life, but all Damon Foxx had to do was crook his finger in her direction to make her tumble into his bed.

What must Damon be thinking of her?

She groaned aloud, shaking her tousled blond hair. She pushed her fingers through her hair as though restoring order would also straighten out the mess she'd gotten herself into.

Her cheeks flamed as she remembered tempting Damon beyond control. The slightly tender feeling at the juncture of her thighs told a story of its own. She had jokingly told Damon he couldn't stake a claim on her, but he had possessed her—physically and mentally.

Using the heels of her hands, she rubbed her eyes. *This is absurd,* Tamara told herself violently. What was wrong with her? She was making a mountain out of a molehill. One night's folly didn't mean he possessed her! She wasn't a piece of damned property that the real-estate developer could take an option on, make a down payment, and then complete the deal by making monthly installments. Her chin rose. She flung the covers aside.

The flimsy satin gown lay at the foot of the bed. She wasn't about to traipse through the house in that. She listened for sounds of Damon being in the house as she moved to the open doorway. Coffee percolating was the only sound she heard. She dashed to her own room, shutting the door.

As she hastily pulled on her underwear, slacks and matching lilac shirt, she realized, though tempted, that she couldn't vanish from the ranch without facing him. She picked up her brush from the cosmetic case. The back door slammed, bringing her erect. With quick, sure strokes she brushed the tangles from her shoulder-length hair.

Damon knocked on the door. "Tamara?"

His voice sounded gruffly impatient. *Why,* she wondered. He was the one who had hightailed it out of the house without waking her.

"Tamara? Are you in there?"

She schooled her face into a nonchalant smile before she opened the door. "Of course. I was just..."

"Getting ready to depart?" he questioned in a low, controlled voice.

"How many times do I have to tell you that I don't run?" she staunchly denied, silently wishing she could flee. "Coffee ready?"

He blocked the doorway. "Why are you upset?"

"Upset? Me? You're mistaken." She flashed him what she hoped was a brilliant smile.

"You're holding that brush as though it was a six-shooter you plan on using," he noted, stepping into the room.

Tamara tossed the brush into the suitcase and snapped the lid shut. "Guilt complex? Or is this some sort of reverse psychology you're using on me? You're upset, so you think I must be upset, also."

"Why should I be upset? Last night was beautiful. We'd be in bed together right now if I hadn't had to see to the horses."

"How are Heidi and the filly?" she asked in an effort to change the subject. "I'd like to see them before I leave."

"They're fine." He watched Tamara lift the suitcase off the dresser. "Plan on leaving this morning."

"Um-hmm. I have a stack of tests to grade."

"Stay long enough to have a cup of coffee, won't you?"

When he reached for the suitcase, she shook her head, stubbornly refusing his offer to carry it. He shoved his hands in his front jeans pockets to keep them from curling around her shoulders. He wanted to give her a sharp shake. By refusing the courtesy of having him carry the bag, she was courageously asserting her independence. Her blue eyes defiantly dared him to take the case out of her capable hands.

"I really should be heading back to town," she said, walking around him and out the door.

"Set the suitcase down," he commanded through clenched teeth. "You aren't going to sashay back to town pretending nothing happened last night."

Tamara bent, dropping the case to the floor. Hands on her hips, she turned around and faced him. "Thank you for yesterday, Damon," she politely began, only to have her lips sealed as he pulled her against his chest and kissed her hard.

"You're acting like last night—" His rust-colored eyes widened, dark centers dilating as he watched her wipe his kiss away with the back of her hand.

"Was a mistake," she finalized by completing his sentence. "chalk it up to temporary insanity on my part."

Temper flaring, Damon lightly shook her shoulders. His insecurities surfaced. "Did you sleep with me to assure yourself of your teaching position?"

Tamara gasped, shocked by his biting accusation. Did he really believe keeping her job was that important? Damn him and his assumptions! Her head tilted back defiantly. She goaded, "There are five other *male* board members, aren't there? Perhaps I'm rushing back to town to—"

"Shut up, Tamara!" His hands dropped as his face turned red. "I apologize. That was crass! Stay long enough for us to talk this out. Please?"

"One cup," she relented, strangely affected by the tide of color ebbing toward the roots of his dark auburn hair. His control seemed to malfunction when she antagonized him. As she walked into the kitchen she fervently wished there was something he could say to allay her fears.

Damon removed two ceramic cups from the cupboard. He knew the disastrous relationship Tamara had had during her senior year in high school was affecting her behavior. The touchy subject had to be addressed, but he'd be damned if he knew how to approach it. With great caution, he silently advised himself. He poured the steaming coffee into the cups. "Cream? Sugar?"

"Black," she replied, struggling with her composure. Although Damon had apologized, her pride stung from the angry accusation. Damon Foxx jumped from one wrong conclusion to the next, faster than a bullfrog jumped from lily pad to lily pad.

He placed the cup in front of her and sat down in the chair on the opposite side of the table. "I'm truly sorry, Tamara. I'm plagued with insecurities, also."

She nodded, sipping the scalding hot coffee. "Forget it. I've been rumored to have done worse."

Leaning his elbows on the table, Damon scrutinized her face. "The past is unimportant to me."

Basically he knew Tamara was scrupulously honest. She wouldn't enter into an affair of the heart without making him aware of the harsh consequences she'd previously faced. Should he be patient and wait for her to confide in him? Or would getting the problem out in the open immediately be less painful? Inwardly the thought of her using her teenage error in judgment as a barrier worried him.

"We're governed by our past, Damon, regardless of how much we'd like to push it into the recesses of our minds. You were raised to abide by the rules. Don't you see that you haven't changed? You traded your father's rules for your own, but you continue to live by the book."

"Following the same logic, you continue to flaut the rules, don't you? Which is exemplified by your escort service, your teaching the sex classes, your being on the negotiating team?''

She nodded her head in silent agreement.

''I reject the idea of our destiny being planned,'' he stated solemnly. ''We control our destiny.''

''Not in Baylor City,'' she refuted. ''Everyone knows everybody's business.''

His hands tightened on the mug of coffee. ''Was your coming out here another form of rebellion?''

Her head snapped up. ''No.''

''Tamara,'' he said huskily, releasing his death grip on the cup, closing her hand beneath his. ''You can't walk out of here as though nothing has happened between us.''

''I can and will. My coming here was a mistake. You knew that last night. You were a gentleman, and I was...'' His hand harshly squeezing hers stopped her from completing the contrast.

''Wonderful,'' he substituted. ''Last night I waited outside your door, waited for you to decide to come to me. You did. You're mine, Tamara. Don't bother denying it.''

She looked at him bleakly. Slowly she rose, disengaging his hand. ''No, Damon. I'll go home, grade my papers, prepare for the upcoming battle over the RIF policy. Believe me, the sooner I leave the easier it will be on both of us.''

''Run away as fast as you can, but you won't run far enough. We'll both be in Baylor City. Are you running to see if I'll brave the town gossips and fol-

low you? I will. I don't give a damn about rumors—
past or present.''

"Meaning?'' Her chin lifted a fraction.

The barrier she refused to discuss had to be
breached, Damon swiftly decided. "Meaning, I
don't give two hoots about what happened in your
senior year.''

A strangled laugh burst from her lips. She couldn't
believe what she was hearing. Her character had been
thoroughly defamed! Damon mistakenly thought he
was benevolently excusing her past, but in actuality
he strengthened her resolve to leave.

"You're too generous,'' she responded, drawing
a deep breath to control the itch in the palm of her
hand. She sought and found the icy reserve she de-
pended on to get her out of tight situations. "There
won't be any consequences from your sleeping with
the girl from Pickler Park, Mr. Foxx. Now if you'll
kindly excuse me, I'm going home.''

"You ran away years ago. When are you going to
stop running?'' Damon stood up. His thumbs
hooked in his belt loops to keep from physically re-
straining her departure.

The ice shattered, Tamara's temper exploded.
"Dammit, I've told you over and over again, *I don't
run!*''

"Prove it,'' he bluffed, aware he'd made another
tactical error. "Unbend your stiff-necked pride and
tell me what happened in your senior year. For
heaven's sake, trust me for a change.''

"Why? So you can play judge and jury again? Didn't you learn anything when you took circumstantial evidence and decided I was running a gigolo service for little old ladies?"

"A simple explanation would have—"

"Explanation? Explanation! Why do I owe you or anyone else in Baylor City an explanation!"

"You want me and the whole damned town to think the worst, don't you? Do you go home at night and tell your mother, 'I pulled a fast one on the old fuddy-duddy today. I put Damon Foxx's foot squarely in his mouth and watched him chew it off to the knee.'"

"I don't care what the town chooses to think," she lied. "But, I'd be classified as the village idiot if I flaunted being involved with a member of the school board. The party telephone lines would sizzle." Her voice imitated the nasal tones of Emma and Bertha Schultz. "I knew Tamara Smith wouldn't have to worry about *her* job. You *know* why she wasn't cut. Well, sister dear, men will be men, but you'd think they'd know better than to consort with poor white—"

"That's enough, Tamara," Damon warned, sensing the inner turmoil that had lain beneath her cool exterior as it began to surface.

"You're damned right, that's enough." Her hand sliced the air below her chin. "I've had it up to here with innuendos and false accusations."

Damon wrapped his fingers around her upper arms and pulled her to his lap. He gathered her close.

As though she were a small hurt child, he stroked her back soothingly.

Her stomach churned. Tears gathered in her eyes. Dammit, don't be nice, she wanted to shout. Deep down in her heart, she knew if there was one person in town she had deliberately led astray about herself, it was Damon.

"I don't have an illegitimate child," she mumbled, her pride crumbling beneath his gentle hands. "Martha, my cousin in Houston, needed help with her four kids when she suffered through an unwanted pregnancy. Mom was having a bad bout with her arthritis, plus she couldn't go off and leave me alone, so..."

"Martha needed someone, and you dropped out of Baylor High to go help her?"

Tamara nodded, wiping the moisture from her eyes with one curved finger. "At eighteen, I couldn't think of any way to put an end to the rumor short of climbing up the steps of the courthouse and proclaiming my innocence. That's when I decided if the whole town expected me to be wild, I would fulfill their prophecy to the hilt. Wild Tamara Smith, Baylor City's resident hellcat. Dumb, huh?" She raised her eyes to the ceiling to stop the flow of tears. She rapidly blinked, but they continued to streak downward. "And it was all an illusion, a pretense. Only my mother knew the truth. I was as wild as a caged bird. And like a bird, as I battered my wings against the cage, I hurt myself. After I graduated from college and matured, I set a saner course. I promised myself within ten years I'd be indispensable to the community. From hellcat to guardian angel in a decade.''

A peculiar sensation of acute relief swept through Damon. He'd adjusted to the idea of Tamara's having had a teenage pregnancy. It explained her involvement in the pilot program at school. Now he had to reconsider what motivated her. The whys and wherefores of Tamara Smith were far more complicated than he'd foreseen.

In spite of the silent tears, Tamara grinned wryly. ''Now you can understand why I can't let myself get involved with you.''

He studied her face. ''Don't you think it's time to push aside all the unobtainable goals you set for yourself?''

''Respectability isn't unobtainable.''

''Martyrdom is. Why don't you be yourself for a change? Or if you insist on accepting an assigned role...be my wife. Surely being Mrs. Damon Foxx would assure you of respectability.''

Tamara bolted off his lap and blindly crossed the kitchen. Marriage to the town's hero wouldn't solve problems; it would quadruple them. ''Thanks, but no thanks.''

Expecting her refusal, Damon leaned the chair back on two legs, giving her plenty of room. ''First refusal doesn't mean the bidding is closed.''

''Damon, about last night...'' Her hands nervously fluttered to the sink faucet. She splashed cool water on her face.

"Last night we confirmed why I invited you here and why you came. I foolishly hesitated when I should have avoided giving you an excuse to retreat. Respectability? Remember? I didn't want you wondering if I'd respect you the next morning. And yet, here we are discussing respectability."

Tamara blotted her face on a paper towel. Discussing respectability with him was pointless. How could someone with a pristine reputation understand the problems of someone suspected of being tainted? Being privy to the truth didn't make him impervious to the knowing stares of the townspeople. Didn't he realize that when a snow-white glove was dropped into a mud puddle, the glove always got muddy—the mud never got gloved!

She tossed the damp paper towel into the trash can. "I have papers to grade and lesson plans to complete."

Silently crossing the room, he placed his hands on the sink, capturing her between his forearms. "You're a complicated lady," he breathed against the crown of her head. "Am I any closer to figuring you out than I was back in high school?"

Unable to prevent herself from smiling at his evident quandary, she turned in his arms. The room lost its early-morning chill. His comforting warmth permeated the icy cloud perpetually encasing her thoughts and actions. Her mother, and now Damon, knew the truth. She had trusted him with the key to her past, but she couldn't trust herself to let him unlock the future.

Determined to leave the ranch with her head held high, without looking back, without regretting the slice of happiness she'd found in his arms, she decided to leave him as she'd seen him during the dark hours of night...smiling.

"Take comfort in the knowledge that at least you won't have to worry about being seduced tonight," she teased.

"That brand of worry I'd welcome with open arms," he replied. His tender brown eyes compelled her to raise her eyes. "Look at me, Tamara."

"I have to go, Damon."

His arms dropped. Stepping back, he gave her room to make her escape. "I'm not holding you against your will."

Her head snapped upward. "But you aren't going to make it easy, are you?"

"Don't ask the impossible. I'd much prefer that you stay," he coaxed.

She dodged around him, swiftly moving through the kitchen, the hallway, to the front door. What did she prefer? Common sense prevented her from voicing her heartfelt answer. "I can't. Duty calls. Those papers need to be graded."

When she dipped her shoulder to pick up the suitcase, Damon was already there. For a big man, he could move as quickly, as silently as the woodland creature his last name represented. One arm swung around her, turning her into the muscular hardness of his chest.

"Next time you'll bring the test papers with you," he said very gently. A hunger, intense and primitive, shone in his eyes. In one decisive move, he swept her off her feet and into his arms. "But this time, they'll have to be returned a day late."

"Unprofessional," Tamara halfheartedly argued.

"Give them all an A +. A board member is never contacted about good grades, only bad ones," he advised, hugging her high in his arms as he entered the bedroom and sat down on the bed.

His intention was sublimely clear to Tamara. He wanted her. Best of all, he wanted her enough to set aside any rules of gentlemanly conduct. She contentedly nestled against the open V of his shirt.

"Well, Tamara?"

"Well, what?"

"No veiled seduction this time for either of us. You'll have to say the words."

Her gold-tipped lashes fluttered against his chest. "Damon, I can't."

"One word threads throughout everything you've done: need. Your cousin needed. The students need. The teachers need. The female citizens need. Your mother needs. Unselfishly you've met those needs. What do you need, Tamara?"

"You," she whispered unconvincingly. Then, her voice stronger, firmer, she repeated her answer. "You."

"Your needing someone doesn't make you weak, sweetheart."

"But it does make me vulnerable."

His finger curled under her chin to lift her head. "Then we're both vulnerable. I need you every bit as badly as you need me."

"Don't talk about it. Show me," she encouraged. "I don't want to think about repercussions or consequences."

"There won't be any...unless we make them," he promised.

A sweet smile on her lips invited his kiss. The dark center of his eyes flared hungrily as he accepted the invitation. Slowly he lowered them both into the downy comfort of the tousled bed. Her arms encircled his neck as her lips parted. The buttons of her blouse strained against his chest.

As they magically seemed to undress, she recalled the multiple knots he'd tied in his robe the night before. This time neither of them had unconsciously set barriers between them. The brush of his hand against the rounded curve of her breast as he unbuttoned her shirt, unclasped her bra, sent tongues of flame throughout her. He lifted away from her only long enough to remove their clothing. But instead of wedging himself in the cradle of her open thighs, he sent a shudder of longing from her shoulders to her toes by intimately placing the palm of his hand between the curve of her hips.

"Tell me you need me, sweetheart," he gently persuaded.

"I do need you, Damon. Last night seems years away."

"I should have claimed you years ago and taken you with me when I left Baylor City."

"We were too young," she weakly protested as his fingers dipped toward the budding center of her desire. Her heated eyes, with a hunger as keen as his, wandered over his sleek torso, the muscular contours of his shoulders. "Oh, Damon," she whispered, eyes squeezing shut as he rhythmically probed the golden mystery beneath his hands. "I do need you."

She scattered love bites on the places where her eyes had hungrily feasted. The low throaty groan she heard, the flood of color racing up his neck, testified to his control being severely tested. Without realizing it, she gloried in the power his response gave her.

Damon flattened on his back, pulling her astride him. Their bodies fitted together with an urgency they were powerless to deny. His hips thrust upward with a wild driving force. His fingers dug into the rounded curve of her hips. He demanded she use the position, the power, he'd willingly given her.

"Ride me, love. Hard. I'll carry us further than we could ever have gone years ago."

Her knees were clasped firmly against his waist, and her fingers twisted in the curly mass of hair on his chest. Her eyes closed as she adjusted to his commanding thrust. She was in control, and yet she wasn't. She dominated, but then again, she submitted. The power he'd given her made her powerless to subjugate. She gave; he took. In their passion, their need, they were equal, neither master nor servant.

Tamara clung to one solid reality as their passion flung them away from the realities of the universe: she belonged to Damon Foxx; he belonged to her.

Eight

The southeastern wind brings more than warm weather, Tamara thought as she parked the car in her assigned slot in the teacher's area. She grinned from ear to ear. It brings spring fever...and love?

Climbing the steps to the school building, she hugged her lesson-plan book to her chest. Her bouncy stride bordered on being close to a light-hearted skip. Over the weekend, with Damon's help, she had released years of pent-up secrets and hidden emotions. Lordy, she felt as though she'd grown a foot and weighed a thousand pounds less.

She was early, as usual. Within the hour buses packed with capacity loads of vivacious teenagers would arrive. The double doors would spring open, and theoretically great wisdom would be absorbed by enthralled students. Chuckling, Tamara opened the corridor door, thinking that the vast majority of the time what she learned far exceeeded what she taught.

Halfway to her room she spotted Melissa waving and rushing toward her.

"Slow down, Melissa. You aren't going to last until three o'clock at the rate you're going!" she teased.

"Where were you all weekend? I've been frantic." Melissa fell into step beside Tamara.

In heaven, Tamara considered replying, but instead answered, "I took some time out to stop and smell the roses."

"You must have gone out of town then, because the entire city limits of Baylor City were under pollution alert. The president of the board leaked a real stink bomb!"

Tamara stuck the key into her classroom door and opened it. "The RIF policy? I've been told the board hasn't made any definite decisions."

"Maybe not the entire board, but a niece of the president told Emma, who told everyone on her party line that the board is definitely going to cut staff."

"That's what we've all been afraid of. Leave it to Emma to spread the good news," she muttered, disgruntled. As the lead member of the negotiating team, Tamara should have been notified first. But good ol' Emma and her sister, via the telephone lines, were the gleeful bearers of bad tidings.

"I don't think Emma would have spread the news, cackling like a hen who spent the night with a rooster, unless she knows they plan to cut staff starting at the bottom." Melissa seated herself in the front row. "Dammit! I can't believe it. I'll be sending out résumés, while that old hen who couldn't peck her way out of a wet paper bag, much less teach, will be at the front of the classroom!"

"Calm down, Melissa. You're speculating. We don't have the final word."

"Calm down? God, I'm frantic!" A note of hysteria raised her voice an octave. "I planned on getting married this summer. Jeff isn't going to flush his job down the tubes because I have to pull up stakes. It isn't fair!"

"Jeff Stallins? The plumber?"

Melissa nodded. "It takes time to build a business. He isn't going to say, 'Don't worry, babe, we can move to Timbuktu.' My whole life is ruined."

Remembering what Damon had said regarding the corporate policy of 'last hired; first fired,' Tamara feared Melissa had grounds to worry.

Bob Weinberger, their teammate on the bowling league, knocked on the frame of the door and angrily strode into the room.

"What's this about the P.E. and music department being cut?" he demanded as he braced his arms on Tamara's desk and leaned forward. "Why is it the Physical Education Department and the Fine Arts Department are always the first to go?"

Tamara pointed toward Melissa. "She heard that seniority was the basis for the cut."

Bob snorted. "That isn't what the checker at the grocery store told me. I met Clare Field at church on Sunday, and she said she heard the same thing I did. Then she added another juicy tidbit. When the reductions are made, they're doing it by seniority within the department, building by building rather than throughout the entire district. With ten years in the district, I'd have been safe *if* I hadn't transferred to this building last year."

Melissa's eyes brightened. "If my department isn't cut, I won't have to move!"

Bob turned and impaled her with a twist-the-knife-why-don't-you glare.

"Sorry," she mumbled, realizing what she'd said.

"Are there any other rumors you've heard?" Tamara asked both of them.

"Joe Garcia heard they were going to shut down the cafeteria, but you know how those Einstein math teachers get everything screwed up. He hasn't worn a matching pair of socks all year," Bob said disparagingly. "Geraldine, down at Angelo's, says she overheard two of the elementary teachers who said some administrative heads are going to roll. But, once again, I doubt the validity of the source." He balled his fist as he sat down on the corner of Tamara's desk. "It's me. The jocks always get the ax first."

"If they base the cut building by building, my English-teacher's neck could be on the block right beside yours," Tamara added thoughtfully. "I'm the newest teacher in the English department."

"Depending on what rumor you believe," Melissa moaned, "we're all either safe...or sorry."

Gene Harrison, his face beet red, rushed into the room. "I see y'all heard! Who the hell do they think they are? Those elitist bastards can't fire us because we live in Pickler Park!"

"Must be on a different party line," Tamara muttered. "We need a tornado to rip out the phone lines."

"I say we strike!" Gene loudly fumed. "Let the classrooms sit empty for several months. I'm here to tell you, those parents will run the school board out on a rail if the kids are out of school two months early!"

Melissa jumped to her feet, knocking the student desk aside. "Yeah! We'll strike!"

"Whoa!" Tamara interjected. "First of all, each of you heard different rumors. The board may not have made *any* decision. Let's sit tight."

Gene, Melissa and Bob glanced one to another.

"You're the negotiation team's leader, Tamara. We want some answers, and we want them soon!" Bob said in a menacing tone as he shook his finger in Tamara's face. "I hear Damon Foxx is a friend of yours. Find out what's going on."

Bristling at his deliberate pause, she wondered if he'd mentally substituted "friend" for "lover." Tamara struggled to keep a calm composure beneath his penetrating stare. Her imagination ran rampant. Did they know? Did they think she'd sold out?

"Bob, I'm going to chalk that remark up to your being under stress." She captured the accusing finger in her hand. "You've known me since we were kids. Do you honestly believe I'd do anything to endanger your job?"

Withdrawing his finger, obviously contrite, he muttered a quiet "No."

"Oops. Look at the clock. I've got bus duty," Melissa said, rushing toward the door, patting Bob on the shoulder as she passed. "Don't worry about Tamara, Bob. She won't let the Foxx eat her little chick-a-dees."

Gene and Bob followed Melissa out the door.

The rumors couldn't be verified or discounted. Tamara decided to heed her own advice: remain calm. She began her daily routine of preparing for her first class. Picking up her plan book and a piece of chalk, Tamara moved to the chalkboard and began copying the weekly assignment. As she raised her arm she realized the thousand pounds she'd lost over the weekend had been regained. It rested squarely between her shoulder blades.

She wouldn't let herself believe that Damon had heard the rumors and played innocent. He was trustworthy. If the board made a decision, he would have bluntly told her. *Keep telling yourself that,* she mentally advised when doubts began surfacing, stemming from her insecurities.

His primary reason for inviting her to the ranch wasn't tied to making a public announcement about school-board decisions. On numerous occasions he'd frankly told her that he clocked out at five on Fridays and didn't conduct business until nine on Monday mornings. Revealing the specifics of the RIF policy might have endangered his plans for the evening.

Now wait a minute, she mentally argued. If she hadn't enticed him, they wouldn't have slept together. In that respect, she couldn't fault Damon. Or could she? When she called him, he'd been outside her door waiting. A tremor ran though her hand. The chalk snapped, half of it falling into the chalk tray. A dark thought clouded her mind. Had Damon Foxx invited her to the ranch to get information from her? Had she disclosed pertinent information about the attitudes of the teachers? Worse, had the entire weekend been a ruse on his part?

Tamara returned the remaining chalk back to the tray. No, she vehemently protested. Damon lived by the rule book; he wasn't dishonest!

The caustic inner voice didn't answer, but the seeds of doubt had been planted.

Tamara crossed to her desk and opened her change purse. Dithering wouldn't answer the questions. She'd call Damon and ask! Glancing at her wristwatch, she hurried. In five minutes she had to be in front of her door for hall duty.

As she rushed down the hall, Gene stepped from out of his classroom. "Where's the fire?" he teased.

"I've got to make a phone call," she tossed over her shoulder without stopping.

Slightly breathless, she hooked the receiver between her ear and shoulder, plunked the quarter into the pay phone and searched for the number of Foxx, Realtor and Land Developer in the telephone book.

"Who're you calling?" Gene asked. "I worked my way through college as a phone operator. I'll get the number for you."

Tamara gulped. Bob had already accused her of consorting with the adversary. What would Gene think if she told him who she was calling? She'd be confirming Bob's worst suspicions.

She read the heading on the page beneath her hand. "The exterminator," she lied. "I've got bugs in my house."

"They must be Texas-sized for you to tear down the hall like you did. Is your mother in mortal danger of being attacked?" he joked.

"I just keep forgetting. I promised myself to take care of it today."

Gene pointed to an ad at the bottom of the page. "Use him. He's the best in town."

Dialing the number, Tamara groaned. "No answer. I guess— Uh, yes," she stammered when the phone on the other end was picked up. "My name is Tamara Smith. Yes, that's where I live. Could you stop by my house today?"

The first bell rang. Gene waved and headed back to his doorway.

"I'd appreciate your calling my mother before you arrive," she stipulated, knowing the door wouldn't be answered otherwise. "Thanks."

Terrific, she silently blasted. Not only did Gene make her feel like a betraying rat, now she could look forward to going home to a house filled with rat poison. Who says there isn't poetic justice in this world, she fumed.

By the time her last period of teaching rolled around, Tamara wasn't capable of conjugating a verb, much less convincing twenty-five fidgeting students of the lifelong value of being able to identify a gerund. Her efforts to contact Damon between classes had been frustrating and fruitless. When she did finally manage to sneak down the hallway to use the telephone when no one was looking, the line was busy. The entire day could be categorized as an exercise in futility.

As she walked past the public phone on her way to the teacher's lounge, she watched another teacher dropping in coins. Determined to clear the doubts that were gaining momentum in her own mind, she decided to do the forbidden: make a personal call on the phone in the lounge.

Tamara smiled weakly as she dialed the number she'd memorized. How she wished Damon would magically appear the way he had a few weeks ago. She pressed the phone against her ear, willing his line to be free.

"Foxx Realty," a cultured voice answered.

"Mr. Foxx, please."

"Whom shall I say is calling?"

Swallowing, aware of how the phone lines were already buzzing with rumors, she hesitated. "Gertrude Schwartzenagel, from Dallas," she fibbed.

"One moment, please."

The second lie of the day lodged bitterly in her throat. Face it, Tamara, she advised herself, you aren't cut out for the world of undercover espionage. Her tongue worried back and forth over her bottom teeth.

Damon answered the phone just as Emma Schultz entered the lounge.

A burglar in a pawnshop selling his ill-begotten gains as a police officer entered would have felt more comfortable! "Er, ah, I...forget it!" Tamara slammed the phone down.

The sound of the coins Emma dropped into the Coke machine matched the pounding at the back of Tamara's head. She watched Emma collect her change from the machine, pick up the red can and with mincing steps walk over to the sofa.

"Tamara, dear, you're just the person I was hoping to chat with," Emma said in an ingratiating voice.

Tamara, dear? Jumpin' Jehoshaphat! Was the entire faculty going bonkers?

"I have this teacher friend...in another building, you understand, who is concerned about the vicious rumors going around."

Tamara tried, but she couldn't hold it behind her teeth. She audibly groaned and smacked her forehead with the palm of her hand.

"Yes, well, dear," Emma continued, edging closer, whispering. "This friend of mine is over sixty-five. Her contract isn't automatically renewed. She wondered if the cuts in staff would affect the possibility of her being rehired."

For the first time in years, Tamara closely scrutinized Emma Schultz. Powder couldn't cover the minuscule network of wrinkles. The parchment-thin skin on her hands allowed the observer to see the bluish veins. Her high-collared blouse couldn't cover the age lines below her jowls. Could Emma Schultz be expressing her own fears? Were the rumors she capriciously spread merely red herrings to hide deep-seated anxieties? Tamara couldn't relieve her mind any more than she could reassure the other members of the faculty.

"Emma, I can't answer your question. The official word hasn't been passed down."

"Well, of course I wasn't worried about myself." One hand fluttered over the permanent waves of her professionally maintained bluish-white hair. She droned, "My job is secure. I have seniority. I've never done anything uncircumspect. I've been a staunch supporter of the administration. *And*, I do live on the right end of town."

Any flicker of compassion on Tamara's part suffered. The bigoted recital of why Emma felt she was better qualified than other members of the staff irked her. She bit her tongue. Her personal integrity fought against the urge to retaliate with the same acid level found in every rumor Emma spread. The students snickered as they repeated the rumor that Emma Schultz had designed the original blueprints for the high school back in 1902! Much as she disliked Emma, she wouldn't voice the rumor. Tamara couldn't spot an individual's weakness and purposely jab at it the way Emma did.

"Maybe we'll get some factual information at the faculty meeting this afternoon," Tamara stated, rising. Unable to curb her natural tendency toward blunt honesty, she added, "Rumors fragment the faculty into factions. Whoever is spreading them ought to keep her mouth shut."

The remark whizzed right over Emma's head. Caught up in her mythical friend's problem, she didn't have the time or the inclination to be concerned about none-too-subtle hints. She dropped her soda into the trash can and scurried out the door after Tamara.

"I'm coming, too! It wouldn't do me a bit of good to be caught sharing confidences with you," Emma blurted without forethought. Her fingertips covered her mouth. "I mean...well..."

Tamara rescued her from further embarrassment. "One professional talking to another isn't a criminal offense, Emma. Not even in the updated version of the policy handbook Mr. Foxx uses."

Half an hour later, Tamara eased herself into a chair at the back of the small auditorium where the weekly faculty meeting was held. The noise level made her head throb beneath her fingers as she rubbed it. The principal stepped to the podium and raised his hands.

"Ladies and gentlemen, I've been bombarded by your concerned questions. Right before I walked in here, I received a call from the central office. A decision has been made regarding contracts for next year."

Tamara straightened out of her slouched posture. The auditorium became silent as though each person sitting there had taken a deep breath in anticipation of the final verdict.

"The number of teachers designated to be cut has not been established. However, the criteria and the method have been decided." He paused. His lips thinned as though the next words he spoke were distasteful. "The final decision has been left to the discretion of the building principal."

Tamara expelled the breath as her jaw dropped, as did those of several other faculty members. The board, in effect, had painted a big, bold line between the administrators and the faculty members. Of the various rumors Tamara heard during the day, the truth would prove far more divisive than the speculation.

One voice from across the room shouted, "No."

The home-economics teachers sitting next to Tamara mumbled, "Our jobs depend on brownnosing the administration?"

The principal silenced the growing mutterings by lifting his hands.

"I will carefully review the evaluation forms and attempt to base my decision on what is best for the district." He stepped back, motioning for one of the three assistant principals to conduct the remainder of the meeting. Eyes glued to the floor, head moving neither to the right nor to the left, he strode up the aisle and departed.

None of the faculty, Tamara included, heard the announcements the assistant principal made. They each delved into the privacy of their individual guilt feelings.

Did the principal know about the escort service, Tamara wondered. Would he see the part-time job as a project devoted to helping the community? Or would he view it as an attempt solely to increase her income? Initially the principal had opposed having the sex-education pilot program conducted on the secondary level because it was controversial. Would he consider her teaching the seminars as a black mark on the evaluation form? How far had the rumors regarding herself and Damon been spread? And exactly what were the rumors?

Silently Tamara groaned. The rumors couldn't be worse than the apparent truth. She, Tamara Smith, had slept with Damon Foxx, vice president of the Baylor City School Board. Undoubtedly tongues wagged. Everyone would believe Damon knew about the decision to let the top building administrators make the final cut. And everyone knew that a board member could intimidate a building principal. Her job would be safe, as she remembered Damon had promised, but her integrity would be in shreds. She wouldn't be able to face her colleagues.

Far worse, she wouldn't be able to face herself in the mirror knowing the rumors were true. The old rumors about her running away to Houston to have an illegitimate child had been difficult to live down. But that rumor was a vicious lie. This rumor wasn't.

In the darkest corner of her subconscious, had she unconsciously used Damon to ensure her job? She searched deeper into the truth, striving to remember her reasons for risking the weekend at the ranch. She could deceive herself by blaming Damon for dangling the RIF policy under her nose. But the deception wouldn't hold true. She barely shook her head in response to the original question. The townspeople could fault her for having an intimate relationship, but her motivation was pure. Love. In spite of the risk she'd taken, she'd gone to Damon loving him...not his position on the board.

"Are there any other announcements?"

The president of the teacher's organization, Ryan Kemper, walked to the podium. "There will be a meeting of the teaching staff..." He glanced pointedly at the administrators sitting behind him. "Seven in the morning in room 105."

The way her head hurt, Tamara couldn't face listening to the teacher's reactions. Before the assistant principal dismissed the meeting, she was on her feet striding up the aisle. She briefly glanced over her shoulder. Several faculty members were moving between the rows of seats, obviously intent on speaking to her before she left the building.

Tamara sprinted down the hallway and ignored her name being called. Purse in hand, she glanced at her classroom as she passed, thankful she'd locked the door and turned out the lights before going to the meeting.

"Ms Smith! Psst. The Foxx is in the henhouse!" the switch board operator warned from the office doorway.

Curtly acknowledging the information with a nod of her head, she continued down the hallway. As she turned the corner to dash through the doors, she saw Damon. Nonchalantly, as though he couldn't hear her world crashing around her ears, he leaned against the trophy case, waiting.

Another glance over her shoulder reaffirmed her determination to get the hell out of the building. Her world would spin off its axis if she was seen with Damon.

"Tamara! Wait up!" she heard Bob Weinberger call.

Damon had straightened. He smiled warmly.

"I've got to run," she called to both Bob and to Damon.

And fled.

Nine

The phone rang as Tamara entered her home. She cautiously sniffed, expecting to be overwhelmed by the fumes from the exterminator. The pleasant odor of a sugared ham being baked permeated the air. Rubbing her forehead, she heard her mother answer the phone.

"Tamara? Did I hear you come in?"

"Yes, mom. I'm home." She hung her suit jacket in the front closet.

"It's for you, dear."

Taking a deep breath, uncertain she wanted to talk to an irate teacher, she called, "Take the name and number. I'll call them back."

A few seconds later, her mother called, "It's Mr. Foxx. He's being persistent."

After the numerous attempts she'd made to reach him, she should have been delighted. She wasn't. Her loyalty to the teachers combated with a strong desire to confide in Damon.

"I'll get it in my room," Tamara answered. Postponing the inevitable wouldn't help. She'd kicked herself the entire way home for doing exactly what Damon repeatedly accused her of doing: running away from a problem.

Sitting on the edge of her bed, she picked up the extension. "Hello, Damon."

"Gertrude Schwartzenagel, I presume?"

A small, stress-induced chuckle she couldn't control slipped from her lips. "A teacher walked in the lounge just as you came on the line."

"You could have pretended you were talking to a parent," he teased.

Relieved to be talking about anything other than their current problem, she grinned. "Are you casting doubt on the sincerity of the phone call you overheard in the lounge?"

"Of course not," Damon denied.

For long seconds neither of them said anything. The crisis couldn't be ignored. Bravely Tamara plunged in where Damon feared to tread.

"How many of the teachers are going to be cut?" she asked softly.

"I don't know."

"Don't know...or won't tell?"

"What's the rumble I heard in your building about striking?" he asked, shifting the pinching shoe to her foot.

"I don't know," she averred.

"Or won't tell?"

The silence between them left little doubt as to the awkwardness of their situation. They sat on opposite sides of the railroad tracks, which their professional integrity wouldn't allow either of them to cross.

"I missed you," Damon whispered. "Would you go out to dinner with me tonight?"

"Damon, I couldn't stop and talk to you in the hallway. You know I can't be seen publicly with you. The teachers would have my picture posted at the post office on the Ten Most Wanted list."

"We don't have to discuss school business," he coaxed. "It's after five. The doors to my office and the school building are locked. Tamara, I need to see you."

Need? She realized the word plucked at her heartstrings painfully. She silently acknowledged his need and her own needs, but there wasn't anything she could do.

"We can't sneak around."

"Who's sneaking? I'll take you to the town square and parade you around. We've done nothing to be ashamed of. We aren't exchanging strategy for a military campaign."

Tamara sighed. "It isn't what we do; it's what they think we do."

"Who cares what they think? Tamara, I won't let our lives be governed by malicious gossip."

"How do you expect the teachers to trust me, respect me, if I'm seen carousing around with the vice president of the school board? My credibility is at stake!"

"Don't expect angel wings as a reward for faithfully representing the teachers. Striking is illegal. The whole damned staff can be replaced if they go to drastic measures to ensure the jobs of a few incompetents."

"Is that an official threat, Mr. Foxx?" she bristled.

"That's fact. There are state laws about public employees striking. Every one of them could not only lose his job, he could have his teaching certificate pulled. He'll never teach anywhere in the state of Texas."

"Is that right? And who's going to teach the town's little darlings? Pack your bags, Mr. Vice President, you're going to be recruiting teachers from Mexico!"

"Don't be ridiculous. Three teachers can't agree on how to conduct a class. Do you really believe they can stick together under pressure?"

"We're stronger than you think!"

"Be realistic. Those teachers aren't going to put their necks on the chopping block. You'll stick your neck out, and they'll stick their hands in their pockets. I'll have to beg the board not to fire you."

"Beg? Beg! Don't do me any favors! The railroad track runs into town...and out of town. There are districts out of state that appreciate a dedicated teacher."

Damon's voice was strained. "Dammit, you aren't going anywhere."

"Not if the board comes to their senses. Did the board intend to test the Peter Principle when they decided to let the top administrator decide who stays and who goes? You don't actually believe that principals were the best teachers, do you?" she scoffed.

"I refuse to continue this discussion. We're both saying things we don't mean. Regardless of what I've said previously, the decisions made by the board won't affect you," he promised. "Your job is safe."

"How benevolent. Shall I announce your generosity to the other female teachers. Forget pleasing the building principal. Go out to the Foxx ranch."

"That's not what I mean, and you damned well know it."

"Confused, Mr. Foxx? Why don't you get out one of your policy books and quote a rule!"

"Why?" he exploded. "You wouldn't listen. You've spent your entire life ignoring them."

"Go to hell."

"When I do I'll have a hellcat at my side, Ms Smith."

Tamara slammed the phone into its cradle and burst into tears. Her slender legs drew up to her chest as she rolled to her side and pounded the pillow. She'd lost her temper. Things she had no intention of saying had been bellowed into the phone. Untruths. She'd convinced Damon she supported a strike vote. Why didn't she tell Damon she personally opposed teachers' strikes? Why did she lead him to believe the worst? On a gut level, she knew the answer. His quoting state law antagonized her. She hated the written and the unwritten laws that governed his behavior. At the moment, she thoroughly hated Damon Foxx, vice president of the Baylor City School Board.

Tears squeezed between her golden lashes, tracking across her cheeks, over the bridge of her nose, landing on the pillow. She swiped at them with the back of her hand. Despondency, like an insidious black cloud, coldly blanketed her.

"Tamara? Are you sick?" her mother asked from the doorway.

"Uh-huh." *Sick at heart.* "I've had a dreadful headache all day."

"I'll get you some aspirin."

Tamara heard her mother's footsteps recede down the hallway. Too bad there wasn't a simple pill to take for heartache, she thought, pulling a pillow over her head. A common-sense prescription would have prevented the heartache to begin with, she lamented. Common sense told her to avoid Damon Foxx at all costs. But had she listened? No. Recklessly she'd tossed caution to the wind and gone to the ranch to be with Damon. The bitter consequence of her actions was a bitter pill to swallow.

"Here you are, dear." She waited for her daughter to prop herself up on the pillow before handing her the aspirin and water. "Judge Foxx's son upset you?"

The open lines of communication she and her mother shared tangled behind the knot in her throat. "Mom, I can't talk about it."

Mrs. Smith touched her daughter's brow with her gnarled hand, checking for temperature. Then she tenderly pushed the blond wave that was so much like her husband's away from her daughter's tear-streaked face. "Don't talk, sweetheart. Listen."

Tamara scooted to the center of the bed to make room for her frail parent. Arthritis crippled more than her mother's hands. Her shoulders were prematurely stooped. Tiny lines of constant pain etched her beloved face. But her mother was beautiful on the inside, where beauty counts.

"The night Damon took you to Angelo's I knew there would be trouble. I should have warned you then." Her blue eyes watered. "You haven't cried since you came back from helping Martha. It breaks my heart to see you hurt again."

"This is worse, mom. Back then we both knew I was innocent. The town is buzzing about my being with Damon, and I can't deny it. I'm caught between my loyalty to the teachers who are about to strike and Damon. Right now, all I want to do is lock the doors and hide until it's blown over."

Taking a tissue from the box on the nightstand, Mrs. Smith patted the moisture on her daughter's cheeks while she gathered her thoughts. There were things Tamara didn't know about her mother, things she didn't understand about her father's deserting them. She couldn't allow her daughter to cower from respectability. If she did, she could lose her, too.

"I should have told you this story long ago, when you were a child. But back then I was still afraid. Yes, a coward," she admitted woefully. Tamara shook her head as though to argue. "Listen, child. I've never told you why your dad left me, and I should have."

"Don't, mom. I barely remember him."

"But you're about to make the same mistake he did…we did. Your dad and I both grew up in Baylor City. He lived down the street from Judge Foxx, and I grew up two blocks from this house." Her eyes drifted toward the pink-papered walls, and as she talked, her mind digressed beyond the walls. "James Smith was the most handsome boy I'd ever seen. He was tall, blond and blue eyed, and everyone said he was a devil in disguise. But I didn't believe my ears; I believed my eyes. I wanted him more than I'd ever wanted anything in my life. And I risked everything to get him. Pride, honor, self-esteem—everything. The day I married him, I thought I had the world on a platter."

Head sinking to her chin, Tamara empathized with her frail mother. The physical descriptions of the men were different, but the feelings weren't. She wanted to stop her mother from recounting the hurts, but when she saw the faraway look in her aging eyes, she knew she couldn't.

"I was four months pregnant with you. James loved me. I know he did. We avoided his parents' wrath by eloping." Her stooped shoulders caved fractionally. "Nobody in town would hire James. He did odd jobs to keep us in food and shelter. His close friends didn't ignore him, but they did something worse. They pitied him and hated me. Pity devoured his pride. Poverty shamed him. When you were five, he came up with a wild scheme to get rich quick. He was going to show everybody he didn't need their charity. I remember the day he left as though it was yesterday. He read in the paper about wildcatting for oil in west Texas. He borrowed some money from a friend, and he and another buddy left town to strike it rich in the oil fields.

"Easy, so...easy," she recalled solemnly, shaking her head. "Taking the easy road, he deserted us. He never came back. James died when a rig collapsed. But I survived. And what I learned, I've tried to pass on to you. Easy roads lead to blind alleys. You can't let others strip you of honor, pride and self-esteem. When everything else is gone, they're all you have left." Slowly the wallpaper pattern focused, bringing her back to her daughter's problem.

"And the moral of the story is that love isn't worth the price?" Tamara gravely asked.

Her mother turned, resting her hand on her daughter's shoulder. "That's how you've interpreted his leaving for all these years, isn't it?"

Tamara nodded. What other interpretation was there? Her mother had paid a harsh penalty for loving her father. Given the same choices, Tamara was certain she would have avoided the anguish.

"Honey, if your daddy could walk through the front door, I'd welcome him with open arms. I loved him with all my heart."

Tamara's eyes were round with surprise. "You would?"

"Without hesitation. But this time I wouldn't let what other people thought influence what I thought of myself. I wouldn't cringe when the doorbell rang, scared his friends would be on the front stoop looking down at me. I'd make Jim proud of me and himself. We'd work like a team of plow horses—together, instead of each of us pulling in separate directions."

Tamara's mother rose. Her hands at her waist, she attempted to straighten her shoulders. "You and Damon Foxx are fighting the same battles. But you're smarter than I was. You may have drawn the wrong conclusions about your dad and me, but you have the advantage of a decent education and a respectable job to keep you from being afraid to open the front door. Don't ever be afraid. I heard somewhere that a coward dies a thousand deaths, but a brave man only one. Believe me, I died a little each time the doorbell rang."

"You aren't a coward, Mom," Tamara protested, springing off the bed. She wrapped her arms around her mother's bent shoulders. "You're the best mom a girl could have."

Her mother grinned. Her good sense of humor flowered under her daughter's praise. "You're only saying that because it's true," she lightly joked. "Now let me get dinner on the table before you get all sloppy."

After a quick squeeze, Tamara stepped back. "Did the exterminator call today?"

"Uh-huh. I was putting the ham in the oven. Since I haven't seen any vermin, I told him to stick to the scheduled visit. No point spoiling the smell of the ham by stinking up the house with bug spray."

Laughing, Tamara followed her mother toward the kitchen. "At least one of us has our priorities in order," she commented. "The condemned woman ate a hearty meal before facing the gallows?"

"Honey, I raised you right. You'll escape the executioner."

"The board has agreed to discuss the RIF policy with the head of the negotiating team," Ryan Kemper, the president of the teachers' association, announced to the bleary-eyed teachers. "But we must negotiate from strength, not weakness. I suggest we withhold services while the discussion takes place this morning."

"What do you mean? Walk out?" a voice boomed from the back of the room.

The teachers ignored their leader as they voiced their individual opinions to the people seated near them. Tamara observed the chaos as she stood at the back of the room. She and Ryan had spent the evening on the telephone mapping out a strategy. They had two main goals: one, get the board to negotiate; two, teacher solidarity.

Ryan motioned for her to come to the front of the room. Amid the noisy hubbub, she flicked the overhead lights off and on to get them to focus their attention back to Ryan.

"Withholding services is legal," he said, starting to explain the loophole in the contractual agreements each of them had signed without bothering to read. "We were hired to teach. That's all we'll do. No bus duty. No potty patrol. No lunchroom duty. No hall duty," he specifically listed. "We'll show them we mean business."

Tamara grinned at the assembled teachers. "The administrators will be too busy trying to maintain order to have time to hide in their offices reading your evaluation sheets."

While the teachers spontaneously applauded and laughed, Tamara turned to Ryan and spoke in an undertone through smiling lips. "We agreed that you would represent the teachers."

"Foxx demanded the head of the negotiating team to do the bargaining." He shrugged at Tamara, while at the same time giving the teachers a thumbs-up sign.

"Who's going to take my classes?" she hissed.

"Assistant principal. I hope your lesson plans are in good shape," he teased, pointing toward a raised hand in the center of the room.

Bob stood. "Does this mean another criterion, other than the brownnose principle, will determine who leaves and who stays?"

Ryan chuckled at the clever way Bob had stated the question. "The building principals aren't pleased with their role as hatchet men, either. Two elementary principals have threatened to tender their resignations. But to answer your question, Tamara is going to push from a no-cut position. She'll do everything possible to keep the staff intact."

The teachers applauded. "Thanks for raising their hopes and giving me an impossible task!" she caustically commented.

"Meeting dismissed." Ryan turned to Tamara, taking her aside. "Watch them as they leave. Watch how they look at one another as though certain that person will be fired, or worse, will have their job. It's an impossible situation."

"You're telling me it's impossible? I'd much rather be in my classroom today, worrying about getting a pink slip in my mailbox than sitting across the table from Damon Foxx."

"You're tough, and you'll be fair. We're behind you all the way."

Tamara added sardonically, "*Way* behind me. I'll walk out on the limb on one condition...I want a ban on buzz saws posted in the lounge."

"Flash Mr. Foxx your winning smile and he'll recommend hiring additional teachers," Ryan joked.

Shaking her head at the improbability, she moved through the door. "I'll contact you after the negotiations."

A half hour later, armed with facts and figures, Tamara entered the board room. She hoped to be seated, ready to fight, before Damon arrived. She needed the psychological edge of making him walk the width of the room to come to her.

Damon rose as she entered the room.

So much for psyching him out, she thought, unnecessarily adjusting her jacket as she braced her shoulders to make a dignified entrance. Despite the short distance, her breathing sounded harsh to her ears. His dark brown eyes caressing her sent miniature explosions across her skin. The short walk exhausted her more than a day on her feet in the classroom.

She stacked her materials on the opposite side of the table from his. "Morning, Mr. Foxx."

"Ms Smith," Damon greeted her equally formal.

He pushed aside the stack of policy books and state statutes to make room for her file. Searching her face for signs of lack of sleep, he watched her fall of layered blond hair form a curtain in front of her face. When she raised her head, he saw the dark smudges under her eyes that matched his own. Neither of them had slept.

"You okay, Tamara?" he softly asked, concern lacing his voice.

"Why did you stipulate my being the negotiator if you're truly worried about my health?" she questioned. Her heart accelerated to a breathtaking pace when she watched his lip curve into the lopsided smile she found so enchanting.

"A third party who isn't privy to prior discussion would complicate negotiations. Besides, you're beautiful. Ryan isn't."

Tamara twisted her hands in her lap. Damn those dark compelling eyes, she silently cursed. The school board had sent in their big guns, and here she was feeling like a kid with a slingshot on a sandy beach!

In an attempt to knock him off guard, she smiled and replied, "You're beautiful, too."

Damon laughed quietly. He reseated himself, capturing her dressy, spike-heeled shoes between his loafers. "Friendly foes?"

Her knees touched the insides of his muscular thighs. The unexpected intimacy drove any concern for the faculty to the back of her mind. Hard-bargaining negotiator, she silently scoffed, melting toward him instead of having the good sense to back away.

His jawline turned a rosy hue. The desire to let his hand caress the silky length of her slender leg tested his control. Damon forced himself to relinquish the electrifying hold he had on her. He cleared his throat in an effort to block the memories of holding a willing, passionate woman in his arms.

Her chin lifted, indicating her determination to restrain her thoughts from following the same path.

What were they doing on opposite sides of the table, about to hammer out the RIF policy, when merely looking at him undermined rational behavior?

"Let's get this over with, Damon," she suggested, her voice breathy instead of crisp.

"Fine, with one stipulation," he hedged. "Win, lose or draw, the outcome won't affect us personally."

"Stipulation denied. I represent the faculty. Should I fail miserably, my honor would demand that I resign." The nightmare robbing her of sleep had been voiced. An eerie calm cloaked her. Her mother's story echoed in her ears. She understood wanting a man more than her self-respect, her self-esteem. But with her ever-present past, she couldn't face the condemnation of her colleagues. She'd find out today whether she and Damon would work side by side as a team...pulling together or pulling apart.

"I'd block the board from dismissing any teacher, if doing so would safeguard your honor. But I'm only one member with one vote. Don't base your personal decisions on the board's final vote."

Tamara opened the top folder, ending their conversation by introducing a chart showing the present pupil-teacher ratio in each classroom in the district. Hunching forward, Damon selected a page with a turned-down corner from his stack of statutes. He listened carefully to the monotone of her voice as she read the statistics.

A pot of coffee later, they weren't any closer to agreement than they were initially. Tamara stood firm in her belief that cuts in staff were detrimental to the students; Damon reiterated the board's financial position. Both sides were willing to negotiate, but neither budged an inch.

At a particularly heated point in their discussion the phone rang. Tamara reached for it, but Damon's reflexes were faster.

"Yes," he answered curtly. His brown eyes darkened. His lips flattened as they pressed together. "I'll take care of it."

Whatever the person on the other end of the line had disclosed, it ignited his temper, Tamara noted as she heard the phone banged back into place.

"The rebellion started this morning, didn't it? Why didn't you tell me the teachers were refusing to stand duty?" he interrogated.

"The teachers are performing their contractual duties. They're hired to teach, and that's exactly what they're doing." Tamara automatically leaned back in her chair, away from his anger.

"We're supposed to be negotiating in good faith. Don't you think disrupting the routine negates the promise of good faith?"

"Withholding services testifies to our solidarity. Yesterday you doubted the ability of teachers being able to stand together, remember?"

Damon began sorting through his papers, placing them inside his briefcase. "Discussions are concluded. The president of the board feels you've broken faith."

Spontaneously she reacted by reaching across the table. The sensitive pads of her fingertips stroked the dark hairs beneath his starched cuff. Consternation pleated her brow. "You realize what the consequences of breaking off the talks are, don't you?"

"The board has an attorney standing by, ready to file an injunction to stop any illegal actions. Strike and you'll find yourselves in jail."

The logistics of housing more than a hundred teachers in the local jail tickled her sense of humor. "The Schultz sisters incarcerated?" She laughed sardonically. "It would almost be worth the price of admission."

Snapping the lid shut, Damon lithely swung the briefcase to her side. "The leaders will be the first arrested. While you and Ryan are singing the unification chants, the membership will be snuggling up to the administration."

"You've been wrong before," she cautioned.

"True," he admitted, "and each time I could depend on you to ship me up the creek without a paddle. This time, you'll find yourself in the boat...alone, adrift." A small muscle beside his clenched jaw flexed involuntarily. "And there won't be a damned thing I can do about it."

"I don't care. I'll survive—one way or another," she reassured him. Unable to watch him leave the room without giving in to the desire to run after him, she began gathering the number-filled sheets.

Devoting her entire energies on the mundane task, she thought but couldn't be certain that she heard Damon whisper, "I care."

Ten

The moment Tamara reported the aborted peace talks to Ryan, she knew from the disappointment registering in his reply that she'd failed. They expected miracles she had been unable to produce.

"Mr. Foxx indicated the board plans to get an injunction against the teachers and have the violators put in jail," she replied when he questioned her about the final position of the board.

"Hard-line tactics, huh? Well, pack your purse with a toothbrush and toothpaste before you come to the meeting tonight. We'll be here all night making picket signs. The board may be doing us a favor by sending us to jail. At least we can fortify ourselves with forty winks of sleep."

"Leave it to you to see something positive in a bleak situation. Do you think the teachers will strike?"

"How do you feel about striking?"

"I hate the idea. We're adults. It's hanging our dirty laundry out for everyone to see. We should be able to settle our differences."

"You aren't afraid of being sent to jail?"

"Are you kidding?" Tamara bluffed. "I've been kicked out of worse places."

"My wife isn't going to cotton to the idea of being married to a jailbird," he confided. "The Ladies' Literary Society frowns on the husbands of their officers being incarcerated."

Tamara quietly chuckled. "Life is tough on your side of the tracks."

"Life is tough, period. The teachers thought withholding services would turn the trick. It didn't. They'll be back at each other's throats before the day ends."

"Or at mine?" she asked.

"I'll guard your back if you'll guard mine," he replied with a grimace. "I'll see you in the high-school gymnasium at eight o'clock sharp."

"Yeah," she sighed. "Don't you think I should relieve the principal taking my classes?"

"Hell, no. He hasn't been on the inside of a classroom in fifteen years. The kids are dealing him a fit. He sent so many kids to the office for disciplinary measures that his room was nearly empty by the end of each period."

They both laughed, breaking the underlying tension with humor. "See you tonight, Ryan."

Tamara hung up the phone. His questioning her about her attitude on striking gave her food for thought. Was she going to rally the teachers to something she personally abhorred? To her way of thinking, everyone lost the moment the school doors were closed. The repercussions would ripple like boulders dropped in a still pond. The bus drivers would have to cross the picket line or their jobs would be in danger. The cafeteria workers would have to prepare food for a lunch that wouldn't be served, or endanger their jobs. The parents would choose sides. And who knew what motivated them. Some would send their kids to school because they wouldn't be able to get baby-sitters. Others would support the teachers. Head bowed, Tamara left the administration building. Baylor City would splinter into volatile, vocal factions.

Automatically her worried eyes scanned the parking lot, looking for Damon's car. It wasn't there. The position she'd taken earlier wasn't one of her choosing. She hoped he realized she hadn't intentionally withheld information from him. They were both pawns in a game they didn't control. To the casual observer, she was certain she had handled herself in a professional manner.

"But Damon isn't a casual observer," she muttered as she unlocked her car and got inside. Her fingertips tapped the steering wheel. "I care, too."

She cared about more than her job and her reputation. She cared for Damon Foxx. Cared? More than cared...she loved him. The teachers could speculate about under the table dealings, she decided. She was going to follow the dictates of her heart and her conscience.

Toss a bone in the center of the basketball court and they'd slit each other's throats to get it, Tamara surmised as she observed the hostility in the gym. All the teachers needed to start growling and snapping would be the wrong word spoken by their leadership.

Small groups of teachers knotted together. Amazed, she noticed teachers from both sides of the railroad tracks communicating regardless of which side they lived on. People flowed from one group to another. Emma and her sister fluttered in separate paths, but from the reaction on the teachers' faces, they were spreading malicious gossip.

"What do you think?" Melissa asked, joining Tamara on the fringe of the groups.

"I think they're going to get violent," Tamara assessed. "Do you remember the Boo-Yeah routine back in college?"

Melissa nodded. "You're going to use that to..."

Watching Bob muscle up to Gene in a belly-to-belly confrontation, Tamara rushed to the front riser. With Melissa cued in, she'd have the teachers laughing and shouting, or they'd snatch her off the platform and present her to the board as a sacrificial offering.

She tapped the microphone to get the attention of the rowdy group.

"Hey, teachers! You're all going to get fired!"

Shocked, the combined gasp of the teachers was clearly audible.

"Boo! Boo! Hiss!" Melissa shouted at the top of her lungs from the back of the gymnasium. Others joined in, shaking their firsts toward Tamara.

"And be rehired with a fifty-percent increase in pay!" Tamara yelled into the microphone.

"Yeah! Yeah!" Melissa hollered. Her fingers made the victory sign.

The first burst of laughter broke the tension.

"You're going into early retirement!" Tamara taunted.

"Boo! Hiss! Boo!" the crowd chorused with their fists clenched again.

"At full pay!" Her infectious grin made even the sourest puss crumple into full-fledged grins.

"The kids are going to bombard the buildings!"

Melissa, standing on a bleacher, shook her fist as she led the united response. "Hiss! Boo! Hiss!"

"With roses," Tamara added with glee. *"Roses for the teachers!"*

The unlikelihood of that ever occurring had the teachers boisterously laughing, turning to one another, pounding one another on the shoulders as though they had already received a bouquet.

Tamara raised both hands, begging for silence. Slowly the groups began to disband as the teachers seated themselves in the rows of folding chairs. The smiles on their faces reassured her that she, temporarily, held them in her capable hands. Her attention was drawn to the back door as Damon Foxx entered. No one else seemed to notice.

She shifted her eyes away from him. What was he doing here? Dammit, if this meeting went the wrong way, they'd tear him from limb to limb. Concerned for his safety, she tapped the mike. A hundred pairs of eyes focused in her direction.

"Those announcements were *not* official," Tamara said, flashing them a wide, sincere smile. "I did hear an official *rumor*, though. I understand the administrator who took my classes drastically reduced the teacher-pupil ratio down to one to one."

"Not rumor!" Bob yelled. "That's the truth!"

Laughing, Tamara nodded. "Seriously." She schooled her face to appear calm, serene. Inside she felt the opposite. Her knees shook. Her palms perspired. They weren't going to like what she had to say. They were united now. She feared they would remain united when they turned their backs on her. But she'd made her decision. It wasn't the easy way, or even the safe way, but it was the right way.

"When I was a kid my mother used to say there were three ways to do things. My way. Her way. And the highway. Most of you will be pointing me toward the highway, I fear."

"Never!" Ryan shouted from behind her.

Turning to her side, she cautioned, "I'll remind you of that in a few minutes."

She gripped the sides of the podium to steady the tremors in her hands. "The negotiations between myself and the board broke down before I convinced their representative to reconsider the board position. That leaves us with two choices: to strike or not to strike."

Her bright blue eyes panned the teachers. Damon, where are you? She searched but couldn't spot him in the sea of faces. Her throat constricted. "I'm opposed to striking."

The stunned faces, the jaws literally dropping, the sharp intake of air, indicated their surprised reaction. They expected her to lead the picket line. She wouldn't.

Ryan stepped up to the speaker's dais. "We can't back down. I'm not going back to work like a whipped puppy with my tail between my legs."

"I agree. May I finish?" Sputtering, he moved behind her. Forcing herself to laugh, she confided, "He *is* protecting my back, isn't he?"

No one smiled, not even Melissa. As she expected, her views were decidedly unpopular. By listening to the rumors, the mutterings, they'd committed themselves to a radical course of action. As the undisputed rabble-rouser in Baylor City, they assumed she would be at the front of the line carrying a torch.

"As your spokesman I have to speak for myself first. Then, if you choose to disregard what I have to say, I can bend to the will of the majority or resign from representing you."

Whispers and jeers made it impossible to be heard. Tamara stepped away from the microphone. She could shout her beliefs over the loud-speaker system, but she didn't think she'd be heard. Would they respond to a tactic she used in the classroom? She walked away from the mike toward the front row, stopping within inches of the teachers seated there.

"To hear me, you're going to have to listen." She paused long enough for the room to become dead silent. "Under the threat of strike, the board will raise its hackles and become as adamant about their method of dismissal as you are with your outraged sense of righteousness. You'll square off at one another like two bulldogs. But who will win? Not you. Not me. Certainly not the kids. Not the parents. Lines will be drawn as faculty is cut. The wounds inflicted on both sides won't heal. Even if you win, you lose in the long run. The district has a money problem. We can work with the board to solve the problem or multiply the problem a thousandfold by striking. I cast my vote for the teachers being united...with the board...with the community...toward a solid commitment making the Baylor City District, regardless of the financial handicap, the best district in the state!"

Tamara stepped back. Her ears roared with the sound of blood rushing to her head. For long, long seconds the popping of the fluorescent lighting overhead was the only thing heard. Catching her breath, she thrust her chin forward. There was no fear in her eyes. She wouldn't run from them. She'd explained herself, something she'd refused to do in the past. She'd done the only thing she could do.

Emma Schultz pushed her chair back noisily and rose. The second hand on the clock made a full sweep. Bob stood. Melissa stepped into the center aisle. One by one, each of them began a rhythmic clapping. Before the long hand could make another sweep, the entire audience was on its feet applauding.

Tears coursed down the back of her dry throat. She couldn't believe her ears. She hadn't saved their jobs. She hadn't promised them anything but a hard row to hoe. But miraculously they'd stuck by her.

Damon silently moved from the back of the room to the podium. Wordlessly he captured her limp, damp hand and raised it to his lips. The unspoken tribute pulsed hotly from her chilled fingers to her thudding heart. Keeping a tight hold on her fingers, he confidently strode to the microphone. Expectantly the teachers shushed one another.

"I came here directly from an emergency meeting of the board. We spent the last hour pinching nickels until the buffalos squealed." He paused, waiting for their laughter to subside. "The board supports quality education. Without a qualified staff that's impossible. They unanimously voted *not* to cut staff."

Pandemonium broke loose. Teachers cheered, hugged one another and clapped. After a few minutes, Damon thumped the microphone.

"That was the good news! The bad news is each of you is going to have to be stingy. Stingy with sup-

plies. Stingy with electricity. Stingy with demands for
an increase in salary. The Foxx will diligently patrol
the henhouse! Working together—'' his dark eyes
turned toward Tamara ''—against the odds, we can
balance the budget and rewrite the rules.''

The applause drowned out Ryan's dismissing the
meeting. The three of them were swamped by teachers crowding forward. The adrenaline pumped
through Tamara as she was squeezed, good-na-
turedly thumped and kissed. As she basked in their
warm regard, she wondered if she had correctly read
the silent message in Damon's eyes. She watched him
confidently shaking hands, smiling.

The teachers viewed him as their savior. He'd
saved their jobs, hadn't he? Several women eyed him
as though he'd scored a touchdown without the aid
of any other member of the team.

She let the flow of traffic spread past her. Damon
Foxx was, had always been, their town hero. Nothing had changed. But where did that leave her? *Right
back where I started,* she solemnly answered. Taking up unpopular causes, caring for the students as
though they were her own, remaining...she concluded, the naughty but nice lady of Baylor City,
Texas.

Her smile wobbled as she returned to the podium
to retrieve her purse. The tears she'd held in check
trickled down her rounded cheeks. Needing a tissue
desperately, her fingers fought with the clasp on her
purse. Through a blur of water she saw a pristine
white handkerchief dangling over her shoulder.

"Did I steal your thunder?" Damon asked as he turned her around and tenderly dabbed at the moisture.

She sniffed delicately in an effort to stem the tide of self-pity running down her cheeks. Forcing a semblance of what she hoped was a jubilant smile on her face, she answered, "Of course not. Nothing changes. You aren't wearing a football uniform, but you're still the town's hero."

"Is that why you think I barged in on the evening? To grab the glory?" His face flushed bright red. "It isn't! Never has been."

He stuck the handkerchief in his breast pocket as he firmly took her elbow and guided her toward the back door. "Everyone listened to you. Now you're going to do some listening."

"Sneaking out the back door?" she quipped, jerking her elbow.

"It's the quickest way out. Or do you prefer wading through the well-wishers in the front parking lot? Keep punching my button by twisting your arm and I'll insist on the front door. And right there, in the middle of cheering teachers, I'm going to do my best to kiss you silly!"

Unable to curb her tongue, she provoked him. "I guess you think I should be kissing your feet, too! My job was definitely in danger!"

"Shut up. I don't want gratitude from you." He politely held the door open. Once outside, he lengthened his stride to a brisk pace. "Don't ask me what I do want. Your ears will be burning if you do because I have some explicit things in mind."

"You've lost your mind," she muttered.

"You've always driven me crazy. So what's new?"

"Dammit, Damon." She balked, slightly out of breath from jogging to keep pace with him. "You can't make me get into your car."

He tossed his head back and laughed. "Are you about to quote the rules to me? Kidnapping is against the law? Forget it. We're going to my house to write some new rules. Rules both of us can abide by."

He brushed his lips against her forehead. Opening the door on the driver's side, he grinned. "From now on, you'll get in on my side and scoot across, stopping in the center of the bench seat. Agreeable?"

A hint of a smile curved her lips. Back in high school this had been the accepted way to enter a car. She pointed to her chic forest-green suit skirt. "In case you haven't noticed. I'm not wearing slacks."

"Duly noted. I'm anticipating a glimpse of silky thigh."

"A gentleman wouldn't look, much less announce his intentions," she reproved, hiking her skirt up enough to tantalize him.

"Before the evening is concluded, there won't be room between us for you to doubt my intentions." Damon pulled out the keys, then folded himself into the car. "It's my turn to 'need' you."

"Taking advantage of the flaw in my character?" she asked, half joking and half serious.

Starting the car, he pulled out of the parking lot and headed toward his town home. He thoughtfully considered her question. Fighting the board tooth and nail and convincing them to take a rational course was less important to him than the battle he faced. Could he elevate Tamara's self-worth? Tonight, when her colleagues gave her a standing ovation, should have helped. But he knew old wounds from the past were difficult to heal. Small victories equated to band-aid surgery. He needed to free her from the past, or he'd lost.

"I won't take advantage of you, honey. I care too much."

In the soft darkness of the car, Tamara asked the question she'd been afraid to ask in the harsh lighting of the gymnasium. "Why did you come to the meeting?"

"Because I wanted to be tall enough to stand beside you as your equal. I admired your ability to thumb your nose at the town snobs years ago." He glanced at her. Her lovely blue eyes sparkled. "Honey, you don't have to worry about being 'good' enough. The railroad tracks have never separated right from wrong, good from bad."

"The rules are made on your side of the tracks," she disagreed quietly.

"Did you know the school board has one member representing Pickler Park? And yet they changed their position a hundred and eighty degrees. Why? Because it was the right decision. Your facts convinced them...not me."

"You could have taken Ryan aside and told him of the board's change of heart. Why did you wait, letting me put myself on the chopping block?"

"Probably because watching you inspires me to have the courage to do what's right, rather than what the rule book tells me to do. I need you, Tamara Smith. When I feel myself slipping between the pages of the rule book, I need you beside me to keep the covers from slamming shut."

"We're wrong for each other," she weakly protested.

"You're right for me." He pulled the car into the driveway in front of a modest ranch-style home. He shut off the ignition. He held out his hand, palm upward. "Come inside, honey. You belong here with me."

Did she belong here, she wondered as she followed him into the house. Wordlessly he lead her from room to room, but she barely saw the Ethan Allen furniture displayed with showroom neatness. His house lacked the hominess of her mother's house in Pickler Park, and his home at the ranch. This house came straight off the slick pages of an interior decorator's guide.

"You can change anything you don't like," Damon offered. Her silence made him decidedly nervous. Outside the master suite, he paused. *Oh God,* he silently prayed, *let her love me...need me in her life as much as I need her in mine!*

As though she'd heard his thoughts, she wrapped her arms around his waist and laid her head against his chest. His erratic heartbeat matched her own. She felt the damp moisture in his palms as he lightly caressed the side of her face.

"I love you, Damon Foxx, Vice President of the Baylor City School Board, son of the esteemed Judge Foxx, successful realtor." She raised her eyes. She wanted him to see the joy in her heart. "But most of all, I love the man, the grown-up version of Rusty."

"I won't settle for just tonight or a weekend." His voice lowered to the pitch of crushed velour, smooth, strong, plush, but masculine. Heat spread from his neck to the roots of his dark auburn hair. He grasped her tightly, his innate gentleness under stress. "Say you're mine, Tamara. For heaven's sake, put me out of my misery."

"I've been yours for the asking since I was a scruffy eight-year-old."

"You'll marry me?"

Her affirmative answer whispered against his lips. He sealed their agreement with an urgent kiss that voiced his need more eloquently than speech allowed. He held her until any doubt of their being suitable for each other fled.

When he spoke, wistfully glancing at the satin covered king-size bed, his voice trembled. "I don't think I can wait until after the wedding," he confessed.

Tamara laughed tenderly. "Archaic rules don't affect us, do they?" Confident in herself, confident in his love, she laced her fingers through his and led him into the bedroom.

Lazily she began undressing him. His jacket, tie, shirt, slacks and shorts were carelessly tossed into a wing-backed chair beside the bed as her lips followed the leisurely path of her fingers. His muffled groans encouraged each brazen flick of her tongue, pleaded for the pleasure-pain nibble the edges of her teeth inflicted on his heated flesh.

"Enough," he mumbled thickly when she pushed him back against the edge of the bed. His knees buckled, but his quick reflexes allowed him time to grab her. "My skin from my scalp to my toes feels as though it's on fire."

She watched his fingers fumble as he attempted to unbutton her prim white blouse. She languidly shifted to accommodate the removal of the final barrier between them. "I could write my name on your skin, branding you as my own," she whispered against the pulsating vein in his neck.

"It's engraved in my heart, on my soul," he breathed. "Mrs. Tamara Foxx."

"Love me, Damon. Now."

He denied the plea by placing his lips to the tips of her breasts. Tongue circling, swirling, drawing her inside his mouth. The sandpaper-like bristles on his chin lightly abraded the under curve of her breast, sensitizing the flesh. For once he was confident that they had all the time in the world to pleasure each other. And if they didn't, he'd make time!

Tamara squirmed, arching against him. "I love you...*please*."

Her fingernails scored his back, signaling the urgency deep within her. She gasped when she felt him touch her. He muffled her lips from further protest. His tongue sipped her lips. She hadn't realized her teeth had clenched in frustration at her inability to hurry him. She opened to him. And he filled her in one long, hungry thrust. Their tongues mated, stoking her impatience, her need. She arched against his hand, her need surpassing his. Her need wasn't weakness; it gave her the strength to say the words he'd waited to hear.

"I need...need..."

He fulfilled her every need with the masterful, hard stroke of his heated flesh. Intimately locked together, they complemented each other. Neither led nor followed. Together, their goal a common goal, they climbed to the height of passion. There were no boundaries, no restrictions—only love.

"Damon!"

"Yes. Yes. Yes!" he echoed with fervor.

Her body thrust upward, bursting into shivering delight as small convulsions enticed his release. He sank his fingers into her shoulders, arched, nearly voiceless, shouted a final, triumphant, explosive...yes!

He held her as though she was a priceless treasure for long moments. She buried her nose into the side of his neck, inhaling his scent, the scent of their lovemaking. He stroked the smoothness of her throat as he shifted to her side.

The phone ringing on the bedside table jarred against the peaceful, replete silence.

"Ignore it," Damon ordered, content to take gentle love bites at her vulnerable neck.

It continued to ring incessantly, then stopped.

Tamara sighed with contentment. Damon wouldn't allow the outside world to infringe on their loving solitude.

The bell shrilly sliced through warm air.

"Dammit! Persistence must be a hereditary trait. Only one person would call me at this time of night...unless...did you give my number to another irate parent? So help me..." he threatened, grinning at the innocent expression on her face.

He reached across her to the bedside table. "Hello," he growled.

Tamara loved the crush of his chest against her. The tips of her breasts tightened into small rose-buds, burrowing into the warmth of his masculine chest hair.

"Yes. I'll tell her." He paused, listening. "Good night, and don't call later to check up on me."

Damon rocked against her as he replaced the phone on the cradle.

"Who was it?" Tamara asked, undeniably curious.

"An elderly lady requesting the services of a young man," he teased, watching her face light up as she realized the call had come from his grandmother. "She was unable to reach you at home. Your mother suggested she call here."

"My mother is a wise lady."

Damon's lips curved upward. "My grandmother just gave me a bit of advice."

Smoothing her fingers over his brow, Tamara crooned against his lips, "Oh?"

As usual, he couldn't resist. The tip of his tongue flicked between her parted lips. "Mmm. She told me to tear up my little black book. She's a wise lady?" The whispered, inappropriate question mark dangled between them.

Tamara smiled, her blue eyes laughing upward. "You didn't tell her my name was the only name in your book?"

"I'll tell her at the wedding," he replied, winking. "But for now, I have to take care of the vixen who's taken up permanent residence in the Foxx's lair."

The Silhouette Cameo Tote Bag Now available for just $6.99

Handsomely designed in blue and bright pink, its stylish good looks make the Cameo Tote Bag an attractive accessory. The Cameo Tote Bag is big and roomy (13″ square), with reinforced handles and a snap-shut top. You can buy the Cameo Tote Bag for $6.99, plus $1.50 for postage and handling.

Send your name and address with check or money order for $6.99 (plus $1.50 postage and handling), a total of $8.49 to:

**Silhouette Books
120 Brighton Road
P.O. Box 5084
Clifton, NJ 07015-5084
ATTN: Tote Bag**

SIL—T—1

The Silhouette Cameo Tote Bag can be purchased pre-paid only. No charges will be accepted. Please allow 4 to 6 weeks for delivery.

Arizona and N.Y. State Residents Please Add Sales Tax

Take 4 Silhouette Special Edition novels
FREE

and preview future books in your home for 15 days!

When you take advantage of this offer, you get 4 Silhouette Special Edition® novels FREE and without obligation. Then you'll also have the opportunity to preview 6 brand-new books —delivered right to your door for a FREE 15-day examination period—as soon as they are published.

When you decide to keep them, you pay just $1.95 each ($2.50 each in Canada) *with no shipping, handling, or other charges of any kind!*

Romance *is* alive, well and flourishing in the moving love stories of Silhouette Special Edition novels. They'll awaken your desires, enliven your senses, and leave you tingling all over with excitement...and the first 4 novels are yours to keep. You can cancel at any time.

As an added bonus, you'll also receive a FREE subscription to the Silhouette Books Newsletter as long as you remain a member. Each issue is filled with news on upcoming books, interviews with your favorite authors, even their favorite recipes.

To get your 4 FREE books, fill out and mail the coupon today!

Silhouette Special Edition®

Silhouette Books, 120 Brighton Rd., P.O. Box 5084, Clifton, NJ 07015-5084

Clip and mail to: Silhouette Books,
120 Brighton Road, P.O. Box 5084, Clifton, NJ 07015-5084 *

YES. Please send me 4 FREE Silhouette Special Edition novels. Unless you hear from me after I receive them, send me 6 new Silhouette Special Edition novels to preview each month. I understand you will bill me just $1.95 each, a total of $11.70 (in Canada, $2.50 each, a total of $15.00), with no shipping, handling, or other charges of any kind. There is no minimum number of books that I must buy, and I can cancel at any time. The first 4 books are mine to keep.

BS18R6

Name	(please print)

Address	Apt. #

City	State/Prov.	Zip/Postal Code

* In Canada, mail to: Silhouette Canadian Book Club, 320 Steelcase Rd., E., Markham, Ontario, L3R 2M1, Canada
Terms and prices subject to change.
SILHOUETTE SPECIAL EDITION is a service mark and registered trademark.   SE-SUB-1

 Silhouette Desire

COMING NEXT MONTH

A MUCH NEEDED HOLIDAY—Joan Hohl
Neither Kate nor Trace had believed in holiday magic until they
were brought together during the Christmas rush and discovered
the joy of the season together.

MOONLIGHT SERENADE—Laurel Evans
A small-town radio jazz program was just Emma's speed—until
New York executive Simon Eliot tried to get her to shift gears and
join him in the fast lane.

HERO AT LARGE—Aimée Martel
Writing about the Air Force Pararescue School was a difficult task,
and with Commandant Bob Logan watching her every move,
Leslie had a hard time keeping her mind on her work.

TEACHER'S PET—Ariel Berk
Cecily was a teacher who felt deeply about the value of an
education. Nick had achieved success using his wits. Despite their
differences could they learn the lesson of love?

HOOK, LINE AND SINKER—Elaine Camp
Roxie had caught herself an interview with expert angler
Sonny Austin by telling him she was a fishing pro. Now she was on
the hook to make good her claim.

LOVE BY PROXY—Diana Palmer
Amelia's debut as a belly dancer was less than auspicious. Rather
than dazzling her surprised audience with her jingling bangles, she
wound up losing her job, her head and her heart.

AVAILABLE NOW:

TANGLED WEB
Lass Small

HAWK'S FLIGHT
Annette Broadrick

TAKEN BY STORM
Laurien Blair

LOOK BEYOND TOMORROW
Sara Chance

A COLDHEARTED MAN
Lucy Gordon

NAUGHTY, BUT NICE
Jo Ann Algermissen